CREATIVE DIFFERENCES

A. LEX

I need to take a moment to thank BBC for doing justice to all my favorite author's books. Huge shout out to Colin Firth and Jennifer Ehle for your excellent performances that got me through so many dark days.

Thanks to Coca Cola, Death Wish Coffee, and Monster Energy for keeping my ass awake to complete my books.

I guess I should mention my family who supported me but will never read these books. Hi mom!

Shout out to my bestie, for listening to my ramblings and letting me brainstorm in chat so I wouldn't lose my ideas. The hours of Chinese food and plotting. For all the feed back you gave me for all my crazy tangents I took this series on, I can't thank you enough. Vanessa, I love you so much!

To my person: Thank you for being my touchstone since before I can remember. For sticking by me in my darkest times and knowing me better than I could ever know myself. Britty, you're my more than just my chosen sister.

My bitches for reading as I wrote for continuity. Val, you're the best. Honestly, you have been my biggest cheerleader and I can't thank you enough. Meg, Heather, and Vanessa as always thanks for the weekly dinners to keep my sanity.

Next, thanks to my kids Aarynn, Liam, Emilyann, and Hunter for making this process take much longer than it should have. You keep me on my toes, and I wouldn't want it any other way. Always great fun when I would get started on a long writing spree just to lose my train of thought because:

A: someone was breathing too close to the other

B: Someone needed me to do something for them, get them something, bring them something

C: Break up a fight

and had to completely start all over... said no author ever.... But I love you.

Gotta take a second to thank our game night friends for answering all my off the wall, odd ball, out of nowhere questions I came at y'all with. Kenny, Tyler, Xander, and Adam, thanks for putting up with my shenanigans.

Lastly, to my very own Jane Austen man. You're the best man I have ever known. If I loved you less, I might be able to talk about it more. Thank you for encouraging me and believing in me for all these years. Best Terry Bull I ever met. – Love you most, Tara Bull

Love has a way of showing up when you least expect it and changing everything.
     —Unknown

PREFACE

<u>BRADLEY</u>

I love to log into my brainchild, one of the biggest online massively multiplayer online role-playing games; *Annex*. Reading the banter in the world chat channel after the newest expansion launch gives me the biggest sense of accomplishment. The third expansion of *Annex, Rise of the Council*, just came out ten days ago. People are still talking about the latest takedowns and the new and different types of characters they can now play.

As I take a sip of my coffee, a message to the chat catches my attention.

<u>CYBIRA:</u> In search of either alternative healer or alternative damage only for spot in end game content. Ready to transport now. Get your trophy and ultra-weapon. Don't bother messaging if you can't follow basic directions.

I can't help the rush of curiosity I feel as I click the character name to find out their basic information. The character name is Cybira. Level 90 female human, Cleric. Without thinking twice, I switch characters to my alternative healer, Thorantik, and type my message to the player.

<u>THORANTIK:</u> I am interested in joining your group for The Council.

Their reply takes a minute or so. The group must be checking out my character online to see if I meet the armor criteria. My assumption is confirmed when I get a personal message back from Cybira.

CYBIRA: We are running a 20-man takedown. We are about to pull up on The Council. Are you fine only doing the final fight?

THORANTIK: Yep.

I type my response without thought. I can't wait to see a group attempt end game content.

Without any more conversation, an invitation to join the takedown lights up my screen. I hit accept. A takedown message pops up with discord information so I can join their voicechat. I type the information in. I am instantly muted before I can say hello or even thanks for the invite.

"If any of you have a problem following the direction from a woman, leave now before we get started again. I hate that we have to stop and kick members out and find replacements because of sexist crap," a gruff voice rumbles out. "Best of luck to you all." I watch as the man's character name goes offline from the voicechat.

"All right, transport me back so we can get this done. I'm glad I moved my meeting to later." The woman sounds young. "Everyone make sure you have flasks on your hot bar and make sure any minions are set to passive so we don't have a repeat performance like earlier, of minions pulling before we are ready." She laughs. My stomach feels like there are butterflies in it.

I hover my curser over her name on my screen. I see she has the title of Obliterator in front of her name. I'd be lying if I said I wasn't impressed. That title is only for first on the server kills of end game content.

"Okay. As most of you know from being in the same Clan as I am, I will help you all through this. All you have to do is listen to the directions I give you when I give them to you. For those of you new to this fight, when I tell you to stop all damage, I mean it.

Stop moving, casting, and breathing. Stay off any yellow swirls that appear on the floor. I have a warlock and mage tank. Please, do not target anything polymorphed or enslaved. I will tell you when to burn those down." There is quick clicking followed by empowerments casted on characters around me. Since she is the only one not muted anymore, I know she is working to boost our group as she explains. "If your character gets cursed run to me. I will highlight my name in neon blue so you can find and target me easier. If we don't get them this time we can try again. I will open the Clan vault so you all can pay for repairs and restock consumables."

I watch her character open a treasure chest in front of the group. A few characters move closer to interact with the vault and restock their character. I left click her character to look at her armor. She has it set to look like basic clothes instead of the traditional high-level armor that is required of the takedowns she does. Her character has long white hair in a high ponytail. A very basic unassuming human. I never could understand why anyone would decide to be a human in a fantasy MMORPG. She could have been a demon with limitless skin colorings and horns or an elf with magenta hair and little pointy ears, or any of the other playable races *Annex* has come out with over the years.

"Okay, I am going to mark the order for everyone so you know who to target after we kill the first commander. There are four groups of five before we get to the actual Council. If you have any questions, I will unmute chat for a minute to make sure everyone gets it out before we start."

The ping alerts me that I am unmuted. "Okay, so Cy, you want me to polymorph the caster on the right?"

"Yes, Shifty. If you can do the right one, Myinnerdemon can tackle enslaving the minions on the left. The other caster doesn't heal so I am not as worried about her, and alternative casters can toss their minions on her if we have to, but so far it hasn't been needed."

"Yo, Cy, if we get this done on the first try you wanna grab some lunch with me?" a much younger guy chimes in.

She laughs. "We always meet up for after takedown drinks at the Clan tavern."

"This character isn't in the Clan. I never thought to apply for Clanship."

A few people join in laughing. "Well, you will have to go through initiation, Hertz. Can't change the rules just for you, now can we?"

"You got it, Cy! I will be top in damage so I can have after takedown shenanigans," the teen vows.

"Any other questions before I pull the first group?" she asks. A fast-paced song comes on over ventrilo.

"What are we going into battle with today, Cyb?" another guy asks.

"Tonight, we fight to a playlist of Glory Hammer and Sabaton," the woman playing Cybira states before the music gets louder.

"No drinking songs tonight?" an older man laughs as he asks.

"Sorry, Glounder, those tend to be for easier takedowns that don't need one hundred percent attention." The ping rings out that we have all been silenced again. "Maybe I will play one after this is over just for you."

I make the decision to follow her direction slower than I normally would and see how she handles the added stress to an already difficult takedown. I really just want her to talk more. I like her voice.

CHAPTER 1

$\mathcal{E}$<u>LSIE</u>

I watch as the characters on my screen move to avoid the yellow swirls like I had instructed them. I appreciate that out of the twenty, only four are not part of our clan. That makes my job of getting them through this takedown so much easier. It really helps too that two of those strangers are attempting to impress the clan to gain membership, so I know they are going to listen to everything I tell them to.

"Thorantik, you're cursed, move to me so I can dispel." I wait for the character to get in range so I don't have to move my own out of the spot I need her to be in. Slowly, the new person wonders close enough for my spell to reach them.

"Okay, stop everything you are doing in three, two, one." I right click to change the number icon over the target they need to be focused on. "All right, resume damage. Mass effect heal from main healers in three, two, one." I position my character closer to the new target. "Everyone needs to come closer to my character so when blow back happens no one is knocked off the platform."

I watch as everyone quickly moves close to my character on the screen, except Thorantik. I roll my eyes. "Thorantik, you are not going to survive that far back, no one can reach you to heal, and you will be tossed off the..."

Before I can finish my sentence, his character goes flying and his health bar blacks out, indicating the character is dead. I change focus. "If we don't get it this time, we can try it again. Just have fun and get a feel for how the mechanics work on this fight." I check the health bars of the rest of the group. "I really think we got this as long as we don't lose anyone else."

Silence descends as we buckle down to destroy The Council. As the final enemy's health winds down I alt tab to ventrilo and unmute everyone. "Perfect job everyone." I watch as the trophy alerts pop up in the takedown chat. The final council man falls dead and the cut scene for the ones who have never done this fight begins. While I wait for them to finish the short cinematic, I revive Thorantik and transport him back to our area. Cheers over ventrilo rebound around my room as their voices come through my speakers.

"Sorry, my internet lagged on me, and I couldn't move quick enough." A low baritone silences the commotion of the clan. "Thank you for allowing me to take part. It was amazing to watch how coordinated you all are."

"That is all, Cyb. She is the general of our clan; she knows everything about this game." One of the younger guy's praises are full of appreciation.

"It is a shame your character died; you were top on damage when you went over the side." I look back over the chart for the damage dealt this entire encounter.

CHAPTER 2

*B*RADLEY

"Hey, Thorantik, wanna come to the clan tavern with us?" another clan member chimes in. "I know it isn't the same as being in person at a bar but we talk over ventrilo and hang out for a bit."

"You are welcome to join us. You have proven that you could keep up in damage if we took you in our main takedown group," another person says.

"When are you going to start leading that group, Cybira?" an older man speaks up.

There is a pause and everyone stops talking. We all wait. "Never." She finally speaks. "While I do love playing this game and have since day one, leading the main group isn't in my cards."

"Aw, don't let what happened earlier get to ya."

A sigh. "That's just it though, Shawlow, that happens every time I try to lead. I am content leading the sub takedown groups. Besides, if I took over the main group what would Clan Master Larrent do with his life?" She laughs.

A circle appears on the ground near all the characters who all run to step on it. I follow. As the screen reloads, I find my own character in an old tattered rustic tavern on a cliff over an ocean.

Their clan tavern. All the characters sit at various tables and hold mugs of drinks. Cheers ring out from the characters. Some flirt, some joke, a few make rude remarks but all of them mimic their human players in their speech. I haven't seen a clan that does anything like this in the game yet. I love how in character they are.

"Play us an audience participation one, Lass." The older man from earlier adopts a bad Irish accent.

Cybira's character laughs at her clanmate's character on the screen before music fills my office. I listen to them all sing along to some happy Irish song about death. It is then that I decide to apply to join their clan.

THORANTIK: What do I need to do to join your clan? I hit send and wait for Cybira to answer me.

CYBIRA: Why do you want to join? She answers me back, her voice still singing with her friends to the music.

THORANTIK: I liked how thorough you were in your take-down. I enjoy the homeyness this group has. No sooner had I hit send then the invite to join their clan popped up on my screen.

CHAPTER 3

RADLEY
Present Day

CYBIRA: Happy two-year anniversary of being your friend.

THORANTIK: LOL How is that even something you remember? Happy anniversary my friend.

CYBIRA:It happens to be a very special anniversary in my life so it is hard not to remember. Does that make me weird?

With one hundred percent sincerity I type my answer quickly to assure her.

THORANTIK: No. Actually, I think it is endearing. LOL So, what is this special anniversary?

CYBIRA:. No way! We agreed, no personal information.

THORANTIK: Oh! Come on! I hate to be the one to have to reiterate, but today is our two-year anniversary. Doesn't that mean we might be able to tell each-other a few things at the very least?

CYBIRA: I want the record to reflect that this arrangement was all your idea, the secrecy.

THORANTIK: True, but we have logged hundreds if not thousands of hours online together. I think some concessions could be made at this point. I mean I'm sure we have both discovered things about each other with all these hours. For example: I know you play a lowbie character when you want to be left alone. I love that your favorite author is Jane Austen. I know you have a playlist of music that changes based on your mood and the takedown we are doing. I know you play online because in your life you either feel alone or that you have little control over aspects in your life. I'm still trying to figure that one out. LOL

CYBIRA: What if knowing more kills the friendship that we have now?

THORANTIK: I have great faith in our ability to be adults about anything we learn.

CYBIRA: Quick fire: Pineapple on pizza? Chili on spaghetti? Coke or Pepsi?

I smile as I read her questions. "What are you smiling at?" My sister's face pops up on my computer screen, and I ignore her while I type. "Earth to Bradley!" She taps her finger on her screen. I roll my eyes and close out the videochat my sister has interrupted me with.

THORANTIK: Pineapple does not go on my pizza. Ever. No wiggle room on that one. I have never had chili on anything before, so I can't in good faith answer that question. Coke is infinitely superior. Are those deal breakers for learning more about each other?

My hands feel a little clammy as I wait for judgement. Again, my sister pops up on my screen for a videochat. "Give me a few minutes, okay?" I glace at her for a moment before I wait for Cybira to answer me. She returns the eyeroll as she hangs up.

CYBIRA: You score a sixty-six percent, barely passing. You will have to rectify the chili discrepancy before I can give you an official score. But you can't make it yourself, it just isn't the same. So, are we talking deepest darkest secrets? I have to warn you, I will find you and silence you if you discover all my secrets.

THORANTIK: / Shake in my boots /

On the screen, my little character in the game cowers before her character.

CYBIRA: LOL laugh all you want, you don't know. I could be a powerful Amazon woman. I might be able to wipe the floor with you.

THORANTIK: That's very true. Okay, how about we do twenty questions? We can ask them either all at once or as we think of them, whatever works for you.

CYBIRA: You want to do this over chat and not on Ventrilo?

THORANTIK: I'm technically at work right now so Ventrilo isn't an option for me. But if you want to get on later to talk that's cool.

CYBIRA: We know the basics of each other. I mean there isn't a ton more to know. It's just personal details.

THORANTIK: I think there is a ton more to know about each other. Life is the personal details.

It feels like an eternity as I wait for her to type an answer. My gaze flicks to the online friends list on the bottom of my screen. She hasn't logged off. Her character is still in front of mine, unmoving. Finally, her message comes through at the same time her character extends her arms out in question to my own character, questioning me on both platforms. I chuckle as I read her message.

CYBIRA: Why now?

I have been debating for months on getting to know this woman better. My track record with women is not the best, hence why I made the stipulation of not talking about ourselves when we first became friends. When women find out who I am and figure out what I'm worth they stop being themselves and try to be whatever they think I am looking for. Never fails. I have yet to meet a woman who didn't just fall at my feet so to speak. But this woman keeps me online long hours with her conversation and banter. My mind wanders back to just last week when a man in our group started pressuring her into talking sexy in chat and trying to get her to say certain phases, for his own pleasure, I'm sure. She ignored him and effectively walked our gathering through a takedown from the random group locator we were using. How she speaks to other people and the way she makes an effort to relate to them draws me to her. People gravitate to her when she is online. This woman really knows the game, not just her character, but the lore of every detail even I have trouble remembering! She always seems to have time to dedicate to the clan and anyone who seeks her help.

THORANTIK: IDK, we talk for hours online and I think you are witty, intelligent, and not to mention a bona fide woman lol do you know how unheard of that is online? That you know how to play this game, not just sit and do small adventures, you can run a takedown with minimal effort. I find you interesting.

I notice my heart is pounding hard; I hear it, I feel it. The seconds tick by with agonizing slowness as I wait to see if I have officially pushed her too far.

CYBIRA: Okay. I will give you a hint of where to start looking for my social media this week sometime. You will have to be paying attention. If you miss it then knowing more about each other wasn't meant to be.

As the message hits my chat, my notification sounds to alert me that my special friend has logged off. I allow myself to breathe. Still a small part of my mind is worried I have pushed her too far. But I scoff at the thought. We have been talking online for so long, I almost can't remember a time we didn't' talk or hang out in the game. I alt tab the screen to minimize my game and get back to the email I was writing to my assistant. I need you to get me the account information for a character named Cybira on the same play field as my main character.

My computer dinged. The reply is quick. I don't know why you bother me with things you could do on your own.

I smile at her answer. Before I can type anything back to her, I hear another ding. Elizabeth Lucus, Cleveland Heights, Ohio. Do you want to know her payment info? Birthday? Blood type perhaps?

I feel guilty using my resources to gain the upper hand over someone I think of as a friend. But when you are dealing with people online you can never be too careful, especially when you created the videogame you met them on. I am proud of the restraint I have demonstrated in not checking her out sooner. I type a quick email back to my assistant, Natalie. No need to get every little detail about her. I am just being curious.

You know you don't have to hide from me. Just be honest that this person makes you wonder if maybe one day you could find someone who gets you just as you are. My sister's reply strikes a nerve.

Thanks for the info. Might need you again later. I look around for a pen and a paper to write this information on. My computer pings again, my sister responded.

I hope so, you pay me to be at your beck and call. Her email has me rolling my eyes. I smile as I type my response.

And here I thought you were here because of my amazing conversation and social skills! How long have you been sitting on this information? I'm the best brother ever! Who else has a great brother that pays them to hang out with them all day?

"*O*ne day I will get paid what I am actually worth!" Natalie walks in my office with a small brown bag in her hand. "I know you prefer to give the impression you are a robot who doesn't eat or sleep but what can I say? I love to kill the image every chance I get."

I take the offered bag from her as she pulls out the plush green seat in front of my desk to sit. She puts the messenger bag she carries on the floor next to her. "I'm not sure if I should hug you or profess my undying love for you in this moment." I can't hide my glee at pulling a twenty-ounce bottle of sugary caffeinated goodness from the bag. The bacon, egg, and cheese bagel is a peasant in comparison.

"I brought you actual food to eat." She dramatically laments as she pulls a small bottle of orange juice from her own bag, she retrieved from her messenger bag at her feet. As she sets it on the desk, she brings a bagel sandwich of her own out to enjoy. "I prefer neither of your offers for my keeping you alive. I do it purely for my own selfish entertainment." She takes a bite and smiles at me.

Natalie is my assistant, but she is also my little sister. I can tell her anything and not worry about her judging me too harshly and I know without question she will always give me her opinion whether I want it or not.

CHAPTER 4

$\mathcal{E}$LSIE

"How was work today dear?" By the looks of it Mariah's phone must be sitting on the counter as her face is out of view.

I shake my head and smile waiting for her to come back to our video chat. "What are you doing?" I prop my own phone up against the stapler on my computer desk.

"I'm making my dinner while talking to you. It has been a long day. I am so glad to be home." She comes into view for a split second before leaving me to look at her ceiling. "So, how was your day?"

"I feel like I got a nice chunk of writing done today. Now, I get to relax." I turn on my computer as I speak.

"You know if people knew who you were you wouldn't be single," Mariah chides.

As I look back at my phone her camera is still fixed on her ceiling. The white is a slightly different color than her walls, maybe from age or maybe from grease... I'm not sure. There is movement in the corner of the screen, one leg at a time a nice size black spider makes his debut. Slowly, it walks to the center of my viewing area and sits. "I also wouldn't have any peace and I would be talked of.

I prefer my anonymity. I have managed to maintain being out of the limelight for over a decade now." I say with a wave of pride. My eyes still watching the spider on her ceiling.

"I'm insanely proud of you, Elizabeth. Truly, I am." Mariah comes fully into view. She stares at me with a wide smile on her face. Her mouth opens but the sound of a door being opened has her shutting it as she looks away from me.

"Hey hon, I tried calling you, but it went to voicemail. I was going to stop for dinner on the way home." Nate's voice is breathless.

"I'm talking to Elizabeth. Sorry, babe," she calls out. I never have to worry Mariah will slip up and call me by my nickname when anyone is around. She is my ride or die. We have been friends since the dawn of time. "I have dinner going now."

She waits to speak again. I hear the soft sound of a door closing on her end. She looks back at the screen. "I'm just worried about you. I hate that you are alone. Wouldn't you like to find someone?"

I fidget with the pen sitting on my desk, my gaze averted from my best friend. The truth is I would trade everything I own in the world if it meant I could find someone who loved me for who I am and not *who* I am.

"I see you thinking over there." Mariah's voice permeates my thoughts. I slowly meet her amber colored gaze.

"I'm used to being alone, Mariah. You're my only family. I don't know how to be with anyone, and I really don't have the time to learn."

Mariah rolls her eyes. "You act like you're an old maid. You're only twenty-nine. Hardly decrepit." Her laughter is infectious. It lasts only seconds before she gives me a serious look. "Please, tell me you are not getting online to play games." Her question is rhetorical. She shakes her head at me, all joking gone. "Now, that, you are too old for."

"I'll have you know online gaming has no age limit!" My voice is indignant. I have been playing *Annex* since it first come out almost five years ago. Millions of people from all over the world play this MMORPG. I decide to change the subject. "I need you to give the sneak peek for the next book when you get a second." I pause, my eyes moving from my friend's gaze to her ceiling again. "Mariah, there is a spider directly above you right now."

Mariah goes crossed eyed for a moment as she raises her gaze. With her attention on the dastardly spider she uses her hand to feel around in front of her. Her hand snatches a spatula off the counter. All I hear is stomping, grunts, and screeching. Mariah doesn't look at her screen as she tries to vanquish her nemesis, Sir Spider.

"Mariah, does that spatula have holes in it? What if he crawls through the holes?" I question her as she tries to defend her kitchen. "Get a stool! All that jumping is not helpful."

Mariah gives me scowl. "I will text you in a bit," she whispers before she makes another attempt to obliterate the poor arachnid. I hang up the video call with my only friend, my pseudo sister.

I love my best friend for how closely she guards my secrets. She is the best of the best. Before I click on the program to lose myself in the online game I have played for almost half a decade, a quiet chime catches my attention. Mariah said she would text me in a bit I didn't think she meant as soon as we hung up our video chat. A Facebook notification glows back at me.

The computer screen sits waiting for me to type my login, but my phone's alert notification light draws me in like a beacon. My stomach gives a weighted foreboding feeling like I am about to walk into a trap. With a couple of taps I have my page manager app opened. The page attached to it is the *Death Burns Within* fan page, a large fantasy series I am the secret author of. I see the sneak peek has uploaded just as I had asked. The comments section is already in the hundreds. So many likes and hearts and happy face emojis. But above the sneak peek is a comment posted to the wall.

ANNEX <u>Death Burns Within</u> is a cheap less creative version of *Annex*. This entire series was stolen from the Derrikson Corporation. LC Lucus plagiarized everything he ever wrote. Stole the entire storyline and plot from *Annex*.

I see there are already hundreds of comments on this statement. As an author I never shy away from confrontation over anything I write. I have nothing to hide when it comes to my writing, all my stories are my own original work. I read through some comments. After twenty minutes of reading both sides of this argument, I decide to do something I never do, I tag the post's originator and make my own statement. *ANNEX*

While both story lines are similar on the surface, they are very much different. I started writing these books ten years ago. I sent off and paid for my copyrights on my own, I worked hard to obtain quality editors, I plan and create all my own covers. *Annex* is an amazing work in I own right. I have great appreciation for that entire fan base and all its creators. But I have never stolen anything in my life.

The first comment on my retort is from none other than the originator of the first post, BA Young.

The main theme and story line between Jaxam and Liranna is one hundred percent the same as Weron and Sharanda in *Annex*.

I laugh and shake my head as I type back to him. *ANNEX:* By those standards both story lines are a rip off of Super Mario Brothers. Are you saying *Annex* and <u>Death Burns Within</u> are both plagiarizing Princess Toadstool? Go home, BA Young, your princess is in another castle.

With that I close my app and switch my phone to silent before placing it face down on my computer desk. Without looking I type in my login. I check the time. Guess I should find something to eat for dinner. It only takes a minute or two to throw a peanut butter and jelly sandwich together. I'm back in my favorite place when I sit back down in my office chair.

<u>THORANTIK</u>: Hey. Glad you're on.

<u>CYBIRA</u>: Of course, we have a clan takeover tonight.

<u>THORANTIK</u>: In like an hour. I wasn't sure if we would have time to talk one on one.

<u>CYBIRA</u>: You want to voicechat or just message here?

<u>THORANTIK</u>: I can open a voicechat session if you are cool with that.

<u>CYBIRA</u>: Kk

He sends my character an invite link in our chat for a voicechat session.

"How was your day?" His deep familiar baritone fills my small room through my speakers. It is warm and comforting. We have talked over voicechat for countless hours. He knows when I am sad, I play online on my alt, so no one knows I am online in the clan, and I listen to classic literature on audio books during those times. Thorantik knows that one day I want to visit Jane Austen's home, and that my favorite color is gray. He knows I don't like cake and I am a sucker for cookies. While he knows me, he doesn't know anything identifying about me either.

"Long. I got some things done that I needed to, so I guess it was worth it. What are you doing?" I take a bite of my sandwich while I wait for him to answer me.

"I just had a dinner meeting and now I am finally able to log in and do my favorite thing in the world." Sometimes I wish I knew what my friend looks like, but the mystery lends itself to my imaginations limitless design. I know he works in business, but we don't discuss in detail anything in our lives. Until now when he wants to ask me questions. Maybe he will totally forget it; maybe he was drunk when we discussed that. Or maybe he thought about it and decided it wasn't worth the risk.

"I have my first question for you, but I feel like maybe it should be a freebie for both of us." My body breaks out in a mild cold sweat. So much for him forgetting. "Actually, there are a couple of things I think should be said between us."

"Such as?" I hope I don't sound as guarded as I think I do.

"I'll go first. My name is Bradley, most people call me Derrik. I am thirty-one . Obviously, I'm male. I currently live in California, but I grew up in Michigan. And I'm single." He chuckles softly at the last sentence.

"Did you seriously just give me your ASL? You are showing your age." I laugh. It has been a hot minute since anyone has asked or answered age, sex, location.

"You're stalling," he muses softly.

"Okay." I take a deep breath and I remember what Mariah said earlier; that she wishes I would find someone. Maybe I can give this guy a little more info than I would a stranger. We have been talking for over two years now. "My name is Elizabeth. I am twenty-nine. I live in Ohio. I am single, but I'm not looking." I add the last part because I don't want to mislead this man.

"Why aren't you looking?" He clears his throat. "Just get out of a bad relationship?"

"To be totally honest, I have never really dated. I don't have a ton of free time. I love my life as it is right now. Someone would have to convince me that my life could be improved with their presence." I take another bite of my food.

"You are very convicted." His voice is warm. It doesn't sound like I offended him.

"I tell you that because you are my friend, and I don't want to mislead you."

"Duly noted." He laughs. "You told me long ago that you are a writer. What do you like to write?"

"I write contemporary romance." I get my character in the game in position for our clan take down. He doesn't get a chance to ask me anymore questions as we both have to switch to our clan's chat session. I end our chat and click the link in the clan chat to get to their voice session.

"Oh, look Cybira is here!" one of the female clan members speaks.

"Hey, I'm here." I get situated in my chair. "Just got done having dinner, so I am ready."

"What did you have?" our clan leader asks, making small talk while we wait for the rest of the clan to log in.

"I made PB&J." I pull out a pad of paper and a pen, just in

case I need to make notes or have an idea for a new story. You never know when inspiration will strike.

"You call that dinner?" My clan leader teases, "I figured you'd have a date or something since it is Saturday night."

"My life isn't that exciting." Our clan take down only lasts two hours tonight. For once we all coordinated perfectly, so had little trouble getting through the content. Most of the clan has signed off and it was only me and six other clan mates, one being my special friend, Thorantik. Or Bradley, as he informed me earlier. I make a note to ask him if he prefers me to call him his name or his nickname. Maybe he prefers me to call him by his character name still. My head hurts just thinking of it.

"Anyone have anything fun coming up this week?" one of the men in the voicechat asks the rest of us in the group.

"I am going to an author *Q AND A* on Tuesday. I am so excited. My mom got me a plane ticket for my birthday so I can go meet her. I hope I get to ask her something," the young woman from earlier says, her voice is so full of excitement.

"Who are you going to see? Does she write anything we might know?" our clan leader asks.

"She writes my favorite series called *Kismet Summers*." She sighs. "Her name is Elsie Williams."

"What are you hoping to ask her?" I ask. I am not sure if I will reveal myself, but it will be nice to know if her question will be an easy thing to answer.

"I want to know if she has ever written a character based on herself either in personality or in life experiences." Wow, talk about a loaded question. I check to see who is active on our chat, and my special friend is on, but it doesn't look like he is active in the chat itself. Here is my chance to give him a hint if he is still listening. I smile at my decision to answer her.

"Yes, I have written a couple of characters based on myself.

Many of them are myself at different stages of my own life. So, the first character based on myself I wrote when I was sixteen, and I have improved myself since then. The character, Bayleigh, in the newest Kismet Summers book is based on my childhood." I smile at my monitor; I know she can't see me since this is just a voicechat, but I can't help it. "Pleased to meet you. When you come on Tuesday, I will leave you a signed copy of my newest book coming out next week at the front desk under your screen name. And make sure you ask that question when your turn comes, it's a really good one." I make another note on my pad of paper. "Talk to you all later." With that I log off voicechat.

CHAPTER 5

*B*RADLEY

I listen to her conversation with our clan mate. She is telling the girl more of herself than she has ever told me. I mentally kick myself for deciding early on to not get into details about ourselves as we furthered our relationship online. Part of me wants to run a detailed background check on her, but the more rational part of me, the one that has been talking to this woman for over two years, wants to wait for her to tell me all this.

I watch as Cybira logs off the clan chat and see the notification that she has logged off completely. The young girl she was talking to stayed in the chat. Her glee at finding out her favorite author not only plays *Annex* too, but also she is in her clan, is about to make the girl explode with happiness. I log out and go straight to my search engine. Elsie Williams only takes me a moment to type in and hit enter. I look for a Wikipedia for basic information on her. The boxes where photos should have been had broken links, There are only a few paragraphs on her life. I skim the information before closing the page out.

I hard power off my computer in annoyance. I decide to grab a beer out of my fridge before I sit on my couch with my iPad. I tap to open my latest word document to write another chapter before bed. I get five sentences typed out before I succumb to the comfort of my couch and fall asleep.

It has been a long weekend of avoiding *Annex*. I have been wrestling with my thoughts on learning more about Cybira. I'm not as mad at her for opening up, I'm sad she hadn't opened up with me in these two years. My conscious keeps reminding me I set that boundary from the very start, nothing personal. The anger I have at myself for trying to protect myself that it backfired is immense. After a long search of my heart, I make the discovery that not knowing her hurts. I missed talking to her for two whole days. That revelation hit me in a way I was not prepared for. Enough is enough, I log into the game to check on today's update. I see Cybira is online.

CHAPTER 6

$\mathcal{E}$LSIE

THORANTIK: Why didn't you tell me you were
an author?

My heart freezes in my chest for a sliver of a second. Almost
that sinking feeling you get when someone catches you in a lie.
But deep down I know I have told my clanmate I write. I probably
said it in passing but I know I have answered that question
honestly anytime anyone asks me.

CYBIRA: I told you I am a writer when you asked me what
I do.

THORANTIK: No. I mean why didn't you tell me you are a
legit, published, and accomplished author?

Ohh, now we are getting to it. The distinction people use to
decide if you are a hobbyist or a professional. The stock of my
online friend is in danger of decreasing in value in the next few
minutes if we both don't tread lightly.

CYBIRA: Does being a writer need the distinction to be a
fact for a person?

I reread the crux of the issue twice before hitting the send
button, and my eyes close instinctively as I wait for the chime of
his response. Thorantik has been my clanmate and online friend

for over two years. I have been playing *Annex,* one of the largest MMORPGs in the world, since the beta released five years ago. It has been my favorite escape. I know I can run quests or help run groups to pass time or to get out of my own head. A chime catches my attention and slowly, tentatively I open my left eye to glance at his purple text indicating we are in a party together.

THORANTIK:

THORANITK: I feel like this is a huge part of you that you didn't tell me.

THORANTIK: I'm hurt you didn't tell me about yourself.

My friend messages quickly after his first response. I don't know what he wants me to say. I told him the truth about what I do, and he didn't ask me to elaborate. If I had said I work in a Starbucks, would he have wanted me to tell him I only run the register, or would he have expected me to type out all my job description? As I think of how I want to mount my defense another chime trills out.

THORANTIK: The other night you were talking to a clanmate over voivechat after the clan take down. She was talking about a book event she was going to attend and you offered to give her a signed copy. I didn't think anything of it until you logged out and she kept going on over how she can't believe her favorite author is in her clan. So, I googled you.

This is why I don't tell people about myself. Once again, who I am has chased away another friend. I shake my head, my heart heavy as I type.

CYBIRA: I'm a writer. I don't know what you want me to say. We agreed when we first started talking that personal information was not necessary. Actually, it was one of the first things you insisted on. We agreed to only use our screen names. I was honest when you asked what I do. I'm a writer.

. . .

*T*HORANITK: It is a huge accomplishment, you making it. You are someone. I just don't get why you didn't trust me enough to tell me.

I sigh. Not everyone seeks fame or fortune. Some of us just seek peace within. I am too drained to begin to explain this right now to him. He said he Googled me. Great. Another person who I will have to be on my guard with, exactly what I was trying to avoid.

*T*HORANTIK: I bet your family is proud. I just thought you would bring it up at some point in all our online hours together.

I close my eyes; I wish that sentence would disappear. The sentiment was nice. It occurs to me that while he might have Googled me, he did not fully read anything about me. That stings. He said I was someone, just not someone worth learning about.

CYBIRA:. If you googled me, you didn't look far enough.

With that I log out. I just don't have the energy today to spend patting his ego or whatever the hell he wants out of me. I write because I love it. I don't write for fame or fortune. The series he is referencing is the only writing attached to my name. My real passion and the main source of income comes from my series called *Death Burns Within*. I write that series under a pseudonym and only two people in the world know I write it. The first is my one and only friend Mariah and the other is my publisher.

CHAPTER 7

$\mathcal{B}$**RADLEY**

"Natalie, could you come in my office for a moment?" I hang up the receiver without waiting for her to reply. I open my laptop and wait for my assistant. My computer springs to life just as she opens the door. Natalie is in her early twenties, straight brown hair curls at her shoulders, and her chocolate brown eyes glitter behind her bright red framed glasses. I respect her opinion and I trust her discretion not only because she is my assistant but because she is my little sister. She sets her messenger bag next to the chair in front of my desk and takes a seat.

"What's up?" her head tilts as her question leaves her lips.

"I need you to find out some information on someone for me. I need to know the basics and maybe a little more."

"Another one? Goodness you're needy lately." She rolls her eyes as she pulls out her phone. "Okay, what is the name so I can make myself a note."

"Elsie Williams." Natalie's gaze snaps to mine as I speak the name.

"Elsie Williams?" Her mouth hangs open and her brow furrows. "Like, the author?"

Now it was my turn to look shocked. "You know of her?"

"Know of her? I am one of her biggest fans." She reaches down and pulls out a book from her bag on the floor. Holding it out to me, I grab it. It is a legit book. Well-read and clearly a romance novel. "I am going after work tomorrow to her signing at the Barnes and Noble on Lakeview. What do you want to know?"

I flip through the pages not sure what I am looking for. There are three hundred and seventeen pages in this particular book. I hand it back to Natalie. "Tell me what you know, and I will see if I have any questions after that."

Natalie giggles. "Okay, Elsie is twenty-nine and lives in Ohio. Fans know they can reach her by email, and she will answer them back. Elsie does not engage in social media; all of that is handled by her assistant."

"Ah, so she is stuck up. How do you know her assistant doesn't answer her emails?"

Natalie squares her shoulders. "Because no one writes quite like her and her fans know that. She does a ton of charity events."

"So, she likes to be center of attention."

"Why, because she does charity events?"

"Real people who donate to charity do so without putting their name on it," I retort.

Natalie shakes her head. "She specifically writes books that all the proceeds go to a named charity or person. Her name draws people to give donations, you know how to use your fame for something like that. The events are enormous, put on by big named people who ask her to donate in some capacity, and donating her time and writing is her contribution."

A small part of me feels bad for saying anything mean about Elsie, an exceedingly small part, I'm still angry she didn't tell me who she was. "Why does she do any of it?"

"The charities?"

"The charities, the intimacy with her fans... all of it." Everyone has a motive.

"Because we are her family." Natalie's eyes brim with tears. "Elsie was a foster child who never got adopted. She has said in many interviews writing has always been her connection to the world she felt forgotten from." I pass her a tissue as a stray tear runs down her cheek.

"So, she is in her mid-twenties. How many children does she have? How does she balance family life?"

Natalie shakes her head. "She has never had children or been involved with anyone. We have many theories on why, as you can imagine."

"Theories? On why she is childless and single?" I arch a brow at my assistant.

She nods. "Growing up in foster care she probably has an aversion to family, but my personal theory is she's too scared to let anyone close."

My heart skips a beat, our whole disagreement was over her not letting me close. I think my sister is on to something. "Why would she be scared?"

Natalie's eyes widen. "Because being so well known comes at a price for some people. A couple of years ago another well-known author's husband was caught not only cheating on his author wife, but he and his mistress tried to off her. When that didn't work, he tried to sue her for half of her work stating he helped her write them by giving her a place to write and funding her career." She lets out a soft, shaky breath, "It was horrible, it was all over the news. And that event really shook Elsie up. She talked about it on her page and gave all kinds of support to the other author and anyone in an abusive situation in general." She takes a breath. "I don't think she had a ton of support while in the system and it wasn't until she was well known that anyone came forward to be part of her family."

I nod in understanding. "How many books has Elsie written?" Surely a woman in her mid-twenties is new to the game.

"She was first published at eighteen. By then she had four books completely written and was just waiting for someone to pick her up." Natalie types on her phone. "She has written thirteen books so far. Four have been made into Hallmark movies."

Natalie turns her phone toward me, to show me the list of book titles. As she moves her finger the page scrolls back to the top and a picture loads. It is a candid shot, not a promo picture, of a woman with dark hair. Her head is bent over a book she is signing, a table full of books and a long line of people before her. The thumbnail is not helpful. Natalie picks this moment to be psychic. She turns her phone back to look at it and scrolls until she gets to what she wants. She hands me the phone back without a word. Her eyes watch me carefully.

It is a photo of Natalie with Elsie. A piercing pair of clear, light gray eyes, thick wavy black hair, and full lips. Her skin is pale, but the brightness of her pink shirt works with it, or maybe the excitement of the moment this photo was taken.

"Why are you interested in Elsie?" Natalie's question should pull my attention from the photo, but it doesn't. Elsie is ethereal.

Without taking my gaze off the phone in front of me I answer honestly without fear of judgement from my sister. "I found out she plays *Annex*." I finally get my fill of gazing at the still and look at Natalie as I hand her back her phone. She doesn't say anything, "I have been playing one of my alternative accounts and talking to her for years. I had no idea she was somebody."

"Somebody?" Natalie scoffs. "Everyone is somebody. Why does she need to have a following to be valued?"

I laugh. "You sound just like her."

Natalie arches one of her brows. "Oh, I see what happened." She puts her phone in her bag, "Let me guess, she told you at some point that she was a writer and in the last day or so you found out she was a published writer." When I didn't answer she smiles wryly, "And you have pled this same case to her about her being 'somebody' and she shut down on you. How close am I?"

"Startlingly so." I study my sister as if looking at her hard might yield the knowledge I crave.

"She talks about that kind of stuff at her *Q AND A*s. It really upsets her that she isn't valued just for being her, especially by people who she cares about. About five years ago she withdrew from events and signings for months and no one saw her. When she finally started doing events again, she was upfront with her fans that people had come out of the woodwork. Apparently, they had done one of those ancestry tests and found they had ties to her and took her to court for part of her creative writings." Natalie leans back in the chair. "I go to every signing I can of hers. Which so far, I have been to seven," she admits.

"Do you still have books you need signed?" Surely if she has gone to so many signings then she has all her books signed.

"I go just to listen to her speak. The way she talks about her books you get the feeling they are real people. At least to Elsie they are; the rest of us just wish for them to be real somewhere."

"Doesn't she just write romance?" Why would anyone want those to be real? There are literally millions of romance books, they are common.

"Something about the way she writes makes you want to believe that these characters are alive in the world, deeply in love, and happy." She smiles as she talks of Elsie's stories. "I'm not the only one. Her following is insane. Enough of a following they made some into movies."

"Do you have to read them in order, or can I just grab any one of them to start?" My question catches her off guard. I move to type on my laptop.

"You really like talking to her that much?" She moves to her bag again. "Here." She hands me another book from her bag. "This is my most prized possession; I won this ARC from a charity raffle a few years ago."

"You say that like I know what ever an ark is, since I'm sure it isn't something that holds animals." I take the book from her, carefully I inspect the spine and back cover.

"It is an acronym, A. R. C." She spells it out for me. "It means this is an advance reader copy of her very first published book. It is what they give out before the final edit gets approved. I am having her sign it when I go tomorrow."

"I will give this back to you tomorrow," I promise her. With that I move to type on my computer, giving the illusion that I am going back to work. Natalie grabs her bag as she gets up to walk to the door.

"I'm going to grab something from the cafeteria, do you want anything?" She turns to look at me as she grabs the door handle.

"Yea, please, just grab me whatever." I answer without taking my eyes off my screen. When I am alone again, I pull up a blank word document on my computer. I make note of all I just learned about this woman I thought I had come to know. My sister proved my preconceived notions wrong there.

I type her name into Google and search images. Her author promotional pics are obviously of a younger woman, probably when she first published. She looked carefree and her eyes shone brightly in the photo. Her clothes were casual, faded blue jeans, a black tank top, a pink and black plaid unbuttoned long sleeve shirt over it. She appeared to have been leaning against a barn, but someone had made her laugh, so she was mid laugh. She is beautiful. Her hair is loose and falling to about her elbow. I scroll down to study more photos. As I scroll, I notice her hair gets longer, she has acquired glasses in some of them, but the most noticeable difference is her eyes aren't as bright and her smile is not as free looking. After the initial promo pic there is nothing professionally of just her.

"She doesn't like having her photo taken." Natalie puts a disposable plate in front of me with my lunch as she resumes her seat. "Taking photos alone just reminds her."

I look up at her, expecting her to finish. I raise my eyebrows. "Reminds her?"

Natalie chewed her bite of sandwich slower, and her eyes turn to my screen. "That in real life, she is utterly alone."

"That is a dire way of putting it," I say between bites of my chicken salad sandwich.

"I told you she has a unique way of writing and talking." Natalie smiles but it is not a happy one.

"She says that about herself?" I look back at my screen, so many people surround her in every photo.

I minimize my browser and alt tab to my character screen on *Annex*. I see my friend is not online. I open a mail tab in my bag to send her a in game letter for when she gets back online.

"What are you doing?" Natalie moves her chair so she can see my screen better. She nods her head toward the screen while looking at me, "So, are you trying to salvage your friendship or are you trying to mend the bridge to make it to another shore?"

I glance at her. My fingers halt as I think about that answer.

"Are you doing this because you realize she is not a lowly player and is 'someone' of substance or do you know she was worth more than just your time because of the years spent talking to her?" I open my mouth, but Natalie interjects, "Are you willing to expose that you are the owner and creator of *Annex*?"

"Is that my only option?" My brow furrows as I ask her.

"Didn't you get upset at her for not telling you exactly who she was and what she does?" Natalie raised an eyebrow as she pops a potato chip in her mouth and smiles.

I nod at her. "Fair point."

My dear friend,

I glance at my sister; she shakes her head. "What? No?"

"Don't raise her expectations. Just be her friend. Nothing has changed unless you want to be one hundred percent honest. Maybe this would be better over voicechat." No sooner were the words out of her mouth than fate intervenes and Elsie signs in. I take a deep breath and send her a voicechat link without a word of hello to her. What if she is still upset with me and refuses to talk to me now?

She accepts it. Natalie puts her hands over her mouth and sits back in her chair.

"Good afternoon." I say, shrugging my shoulders at my sister when she moves her hand to her forehead. Gesturing that I sound stupid.

"Um.... Hi. Am I to assume you have actually read up on me now?" Her tone is light, but her guard is up.

"I have." I lower my voice. "You are impressive." She doesn't say anything. I click to make sure she is still in our chat. "Do you still want to be friends?" I close my eyes as I wait for her to speak. When she doesn't, I look at my sister. She types on her phone and holds it up to me.

Do you want to be her friend or are you hoping this might go further than friendship?

I point to the latter. I like how easy I can talk to her when we are doing assignments in the game together. She is witty and fun. After looking her up I can't forget how beautiful she is. I'm only human. My sister types something else on her phone and shows me the screen again.

Tell her you are sorry for how you reacted earlier. That you thought she was interesting before you looked her up.

I nod at her. "I am sorry, Elsie." I have never wished for videochat in my life but in this moment I do. Finally, she speaks.

"Elizabeth." She softly says, "Most people call me Elizabeth."

"Since I know more about you, I want to tell you something." I look at the ceiling as if looking for a sign that this bit of information about me is going to go over ok with this woman, Natalie nods but has a look of shock and anticipation in her eyes. "I am the owner and creator of *Annex*."

Again, my office is plunged into heavy silence as we both wait to see what she says. Minutes pass, my tie feels too tight around my neck.

"I have to get to a meeting..." She finally speaks but she hesitates, "That isn't entirely true, I really need to think about this new information." Her voice is strong, I like how breathless she sounds. Before I can say anything, "Why are you telling me this?"

"I want you to know something important about me, so the field is even," I answer as honestly as I can. I see my sister purse her lips.

"So, are we playing a game or are you trying to see if claiming something like that will make me fall instantly in love with you?" Her voice chills my office as her tone fills the space.

Without saying anything I open a tab to transfer her character an epic exclusive item from last year's convention *Annex* sponsored.

A minute passes. I can see she opened it. "So, again, why are you telling me this?" She still sounds angry.

"I find you enchanting." It is the most honest answer I can give her.

"Bradley, I need some time to process this." Her answer is like ice cold water thrown on me in the middle of winter. She logs out of the chat before I can say anything.

"You are seriously awkward, brother." Natalie shakes her head. "You need some lessons on how to get a girl. Have you ever been turned down after someone finds out who you are?"

I take a moment to think back over the course of my life, "Not that I can remember." An idea forms in my head, "Hey, could you use an escort to your book signing tomorrow?"

Natalie's eyes widen, "Oh, that is a very good plan!"

"We will get there when they open so we are there for the whole event." I pick up my phone, type the Barnes and Noble into the search, and tap to call. "I would like to request two seats for tomorrows *Q AND A* with Elsie Williams."

"Sir, seating for that event is first come first serve," a woman answers.

"I need to speak to your manager." I wait to be transferred.

"Hello? This is Mr. Antik, how can I help you?" a man picks up and speaks.

"Yes, hello, I am Mr. Derrikson. I need to secure two seats for the *Q AND A* tomorrow with Ms. Williams." I wait for a second, "I am willing to do you a solid if you help me out. I own Derrikson entertainment."

"No problem, sir!" The man said with a little too much excitement. "If you have any book needs please call me directly and I will make sure to handle it exclusively. Now, where would you like to sit?"

"Toward the middle on the end please," I answer. I don't want to be seen until I am ready to expose myself. "Also, I need to ensure no one knows I am in the building or that I called at all."

"Absolutely, sir. I will take care of everything." He pauses. "Is there anything else I can help you with today?"

I think for a moment. "Yes, I need to get my hands on everything Ms. Williams has written."

"Would you also like the movie adaptations?" Mr. Antik is loudly typing on his end. "And what format would you like these books in?"

"All." I answer without thinking. "How long will it take you to get me all of that?"

"I can personally deliver these to you today, sir."

"Excellent, I will make sure there is a visitor badge ready at receiving for you." I quickly hang up.

"You know if we are going when they open, we would be able to pick our seats and we will be insanely early!" Natalie complains.

"Maybe I will get a chance to see her before the event." I can't help but be excited.

CHAPTER 8

$\mathcal{E}$LSIE

I quickly switch my characters, so I am now playing a very low level, non-affiliated character. "Alexa, shuffle my playlist my music."

"Shuffling your playlist *my music* on Amazon music." A melancholy country song starts to play at full volume in my office. My heart immediately feels heavy. I let the sad sensation sweep over my whole self, it feels right considering what I just learned.

A few songs pass on my playlist when my messenger pops up on my computer requesting a videochat with Mariah I don't stop my music as I click accept.

"Oh no. If you are listening to Sabaton something must have you in a mood. Wanna talk about it?" Her hand is under her chin as she leans on her desk to look at her camera and talk to me.

"I have a friend on *Annex* that I have been talking to for two years. We never discuss personal details, ever. But lately, he has decided he wants to know more about me."

Mariah's grin is loving and instant. "I like where this is going." There is a short pause. "Elizabeth is this the character you are always talking to me about? The one you log on just to talk to?"

"Yes. He knows my name now, so he looked me up." I take a

deep breath. "And now that he knows more about who I am, now he is interested. He was actually mad at me for not telling him up front." I make air quotes as I keep talking, "I'm a *real* author."

Mariah makes a face, now she understands. "Elizabeth, not everyone words things perfectly when they are hurt or in a bit of shock." She tries to find something to use to excuse him. "Did he ask to get to know you before he found out you are an author or after?"

I take a second to reflect. "Before." Now, to drop another bomb on her. "He's the owner and creator of *Annex*."

Mariah's mouth opens and doesn't close as she processes what I just said. "Well, at least he has his own money, right? That game has like hundreds of players, isn't that what you told me?"

"Millions of people play this game."

"Then you are perfectly matched!" She claps her hands.

A relationship with someone like that outside of the game just is not sustainable. He has to be a billionaire. Which means he is in the public eye in some capacity. If I were with him, I would be in the limelight as well. It would be expected of me. I would be quieted and censored. I am not interested in that type of life. A soft shudder slithers down my spine at the thought of my name and photo being on anything Mariah's family might see.

"Elizabeth!" Mariah is yelling at me.

"Sorry. I was reading a challenge in the game." I try to cover my errant thoughts.

"You know you can't lie to me," she softly chides.

I take a deep breath. "It wouldn't work outside in the real world."

"What does it hurt to just talk to him?"

"I gotta go." I look at her. "What time am I supposed to be at the *Q AND A* tomorrow?"

"It starts at six, so be there around five unless you want to shop a little, then make it whenever you want." She giggles. Before I can ask her, she says, "I will be there when they open to help them coordinate and set up."

I nod. "I love you most," I tell her.

"One day, I hope you can say that to someone else." She smiles. "I love you too, water sister."

"Like blood," I answer. With that we hang up.

I click to open my bag in game.

To: THORANTIK

I'm not sure how you want me to address you. Bradley? Derrik? Thorantik? I need to get a few things out in the open and I have been told I am more eloquent in print. Probably because I can take back the words I type, whereas, once spoken, words cannot be undone.

You need to search your own heart on if you want to continue down this path, once started you cannot put the genie back in the lamp. Once all is known, the damage to what we have now will be done.

So, to help you think on it I will give you my thoughts. First off, I am not going to google you. That I know of, you have never lied to me. Though we have not learned of our details, in the game you have always had my back and have always been quick to come to my defense if I ever needed it. I will take your word at face value until it is proven that I shouldn't. The problem is, I am to deduce that you are exponentially wealthy. While that might be a wildly played out trope, I am not a woman who pines to find a prince to save her. I am endlessly grateful for all the people who make it so I can live my life and do what I love most. But I have lived most of my life being alone, I love my anonymity. I rely on it.

I love being in charge of my life. I am used to it. I prefer it. I don't want to be censored or owned. Relationships that go real life and stop being online only tend to crash and burn. Even as a child I never dreamed of a wedding, having a marriage, or a family of my own. All I am is writing, it is my entire reason for being.

I told you upfront I am not looking. I was one hundred percent honest. Learning about each other at this point is only going to cause feelings one way or the other. Good answer on the pineapple, that would have meant one thousand confirmation you are a sociopath and no more answers would have been given to you.

At this point I should also say, I am not a robot. I am only human and of course I have moments of extreme loneliness and in the past two years it has crossed my mind to reach out and see if this could go further. But then a call comes in that should only take a few minutes and it ends up taking fourteen hours, thus ruining any plans I might have had. At those times I am reminded that my life is hectic and not suitable for any relationships.

Hopefully this doesn't impede our current relationship and we can continue to be friends. If you think this all over and still want to ask questions then I won't stop you, and I will answer any of them.

Hope to talk to you soon.

Elizabeth/ CYBIRA

I take a deep breath as I hit send.

Now, the dreaded wait sets in. What if he reads this and stops talking to me or ignores me? My heart hurts just thinking of it. It is still early but I decide to go to bed. I'm too anxious to sit and wait for him to sign in to read it.

CHAPTER 9

BRADLEY

I left work as soon as soon as Mr. Antik brought me the items I requested from his store. I have been engrossed in the first book in the Kismet Summers series. Her writing is light and funny. Her characters are in their mid to late twenties. Hard to believe a teenager wrote this. It is charming. I can see why her writing was picked up from something like Hallmark. I finish the first book just as it starts to get dark out. I hear my phone going off.

"Hello?" I answer as I make my way to my kitchen to find something to eat.

"Sir, we have a game ticket in from a player but none of the technicians are able to fix it. Can you log in and see if there is something you can do?" My head of support, Cory, sounds frazzled.

"Sure, no problem." I grab the pizza box out of my fridge and carry it to my office. *Annex* is already pulled up, waiting for me to login.

"Thank you, sir. Do you want me to stay on the phone?" He sounds nervous.

"No, if I need you, I will just call you back." I hit enter after typing in my password. I click on my administrator character to access the ticket put in. It takes me a better part of twenty minutes to get the account fixed. After I got him sorted and happy, I log out of my admin character and without a second thought I log my favorite alternate character.

I am disappointed Elsie is not on. But I have a mail icon on my bag. I click on it to open. My heartrate kicks up a few notches as I see it is from CYBIRA. Elsie sent me a letter in game. As I read it, my heartrate slows. I reread it; I feel like my office is suddenly too small. I do the only thing I can think of, I call my sister.

"What?" she answers, her tone playful and not perturbed.

"I am going to read you something and I need your opinion." I wait for her to say something, but Natalie stays silent, waiting. I read her the letter. She is silent for a long minute.

"Okay, what is your first thought on it?" she asks me.

"My first inclination is to run an extensive background check on her!" I exclaim, annoyed that she isn't telling me what to do.

"That is not a good idea." She warns, "I think you should stick to your plan of going to the signing *Q AND A* tomorrow."

"Yea," I concede.

"Did you get around to reading any of the books you got today?" Natalie sounds excited.

"I read the first one." I smile. "Are you sure she wrote that..."

"She wrote it when she was sixteen," she interjects before I can finish my sentence.

"It is pretty amazing," I admit. "Her writing perfectly makes a scene in my head. I feel like this could be a graphic novel."

Natalie bursts into laughter. "That guy from the bookstore must have only brought her regular books." Her laugh finally stopped. "Her books are all converted to graphic novels."

"Really?" That is unusual.

"Yea, she heard some younger fans lament that they wished her books were graphic novels because it is hard for them to keep up with typical chapter books. So, Elsie, made sure they could enjoy her books in the format they preferred." She takes a second and continues, "She said it only made sense to accommodate them too since everything else is made into audio books, movies, large print, and even Braille. She also makes sure her books are available in a multitude of languages."

"You sound like you are in love with her, yourself," I tease.

"I admire her. She is a great role model."

"Okay, I will see you tomorrow. What time does this start?" I close out my game.

"It starts at six PM." She waits for me to speak.

"Okay, I will head over around ten."

"AM!" Natalie's voice is shrill.

"Yea, I can eat there all day and drink coffee while I read some more."

"Okay, I will see you when I see you. I am not in love with her like you are, so I will not be wasting my entire day waiting for her." She laughs.

"I'm not in love with her." The denial lacks conviction even to my own ears. "I just have to know some more about her."

"Sure, sure Romeo." She hangs up before I can retort.

I shake my head at her lingering words. "I just like her a lot." I answer the silence of my office. My stomach feels like it is full of weights. I am seeing Elsie tomorrow. With my own eyes. Hearing her voice in person. What should I wear to something like this? I look at my phone on the filing cabinet next to my desk, weighing out if I should call my sister back and ask her what I need to wear. But her words replay in my mind. I'm already a mess over this woman.

I grab my iPad out of my desk drawer and open it. The decision to use this time to get some more writing done for *Annex* seems like the best option for me right now.

CHAPTER 10

ELSIE

The sound of my ringtone wakes me up. The sun hasn't kissed the horizon yet, it is just thinking of rising itself. With a groan I answer it.

"Hello?" I didn't even check to see who was calling.

"Sarah?" A frail woman asks.

"No ma'am, this is not Sarah. I'm afraid you have the wrong number."

"This number used to belong to my daughter. She died almost twenty years ago," the woman explained. "Today would have been her forty-fifth birthday."

I sit up in my bed and glance at the clock on the wall over my closet door; 6:13. I say the only logical thing I can think of. "Tell me your most favorite memory of Sarah."

There is a muffle on the other end. She is crying softly, and her voice is somber as she speaks. "Sarah was the only girl I had. She is the youngest of my four children. Her brothers have all grown up and made their own lives." She takes a second to gather herself. "I live alone, and I feel like the world moved on without me."

"I can relate to that," I tell her as I get up out of my bad. "Tell me more. I have all the time you need." She hesitates. "You called because you miss your daughter. Since I answered I think it is no mistake we were meant to speak."

"Your logic sounds like my Sarah's." She laughs softly. "My name is Evaline."

"Pleasure to make your acquaintance. Please, call me Elizabeth." I pull my long silk robe around me to cover my nightgown. I make my way to the kitchen. The little house I rented for the next week and a half is cozy and fully furnished. "Where do you stay, Evaline?"

"I stay at Huntington Court off Princeton Pike," she answers, her voice soft but strong.

"And do you get many visitors?" I start my coffee.

"My sons come once or twice a year when they are in town." She pauses, then continues, "What is it you do? Do you have a partner or children?"

I give a small laugh as I pour my coffee. "I have neither I am sorry to disappoint. My parents died when I was very little, and I had no family to live with. I'm afraid I am all alone except for my dearest friend, Mariah. She is getting married at the end of the week and will no doubt start her own family soon." I frown at the idea of being all alone in my adult life too, now that my friend is soon to be married. I shove the idea away, "But I am an author. I write love stories to warm people's hearts."

"What a wonderful thing. My days are now filled with reading and puzzles." Evaline's voice holds a touch of melancholy.

I grab my iPad off the charger on my nightstand and look up Huntington Court. I see she is about forty minutes from my home in Ohio. "Why are you in such a place, Evaline?"

"To be perfectly honest, my children did not want to worry about me, and I had no reason to burden them."

"Are you unable to care for yourself? You don't sound like you are older than maybe your sixties. And that is only because you have already revealed that you have a child that is in their forties." I add the last part quickly because she doesn't sound old at all.

Sad; she sounds sad and lonely. I know those sentiments all too well.

"I am seventy-two." She chuckles, "How old are you my dear?"

"I am twenty-nine." I drink my coffee quickly. A pleasant pause that seems to be more like a warm hug than an awkward moment. "So, what are your plans for today, Evaline?"

"Well, let me see what is on the calendar for today at this facility." I hear rustling pages. "Ah, today is bingo and then we are going to watch *Rent*...hmmmm, I'm not sure what that is."

"It's a musical." I laugh as I get up from the small table and head to my closet. I didn't bring many clothes, but I have to figure out what to wear today. "Evaline, do you own an iPad or a kindle, or any kind of tablet?"

"I use my iPad for reading and games." I hear someone on her end talk to her. She mumbles something to them.

"Would you like to read one of my books?" I offer her as I pull out a pair of faded jeans. Those are a definite must for a signing. If I have to sit for that long I am going to be comfortable.

"I would love to read something heartwarming." There is some tapping on her end. "Can I text you my email?"

"Oh, that sounds perfect."

"What are your plans for today, Elizabeth?"

"I have a book signing today in the evening, but I am going to head out and do a little shopping while I am away from home." I grab a gray tank top out of the closet and a black button-down short sleeve shirt to use as a cover up.

"That sounds exciting." She takes a deep breath. "I think I am boring you to death."

"Absolutely not." I close my closet door. "You are a most welcome presence right now."

"Thank you for talking to me today, Elizabeth. It has been a long time since I have met someone new or had any new conversation."

"Can you do me a favor?" I ask her without thinking of what I am asking her.

"You can, if I can oblige then I will!" Evaline sounds sincere.

"Do you promise to call me whenever the mood strikes? If for any reason I don't answer just leave me a message and I promise to call you back."

"I can, but why on earth would you want me to?" She sounds shocked and confused.

"It has been a very long time since I have had someone new to talk to and I enjoy your conversation." It was the most honest thing I have ever said to a stranger.

"Absolutely, I will but I will wait until after I have breakfast. Give you another hour or two of sleep." Her voice is more hopeful than it was.

"Perfect, I look forward to it." I move to make my bed, "I hope you enjoy your day, Evaline."

"You too. Best of luck today on your signing." With that she disconnects the line. I glance at my phone as I put it down and smile. What are the odds of something like that happening? I gather my clothes to head into the bathroom to take my shower and get ready for my day.

CHAPTER 11

$\mathcal{B}$RADLEY

"Okay, I admit it, I need help!" I hate admitting to my sister that I am over thinking seeing this woman but here I am.

She's laughing at me. "Okay, what do you need?"

Silence. I don't know if I can bring myself to utter that I don't know what to wear to see a woman I have been talking to for two years and slowly falling in love with.

"Bradley!" Natalie yells, I hate when she uses my real name. She sounds like Mom when she does it. Thankfully, it isn't often she needs to.

"Huh? Oh, okay. What should I wear?" I grimace at my phone; she can't see me as we are not on video, but I am worried about her answer and her reaction to me being such a mess.

"Aww my big brother is worried about how his first meeting will be with his online girlfriend."

"Hey! She's your favorite author!" My tone cuts all humor in this moment.

"Oh my god! You're right! If you really hit it off, she could be like one of my new best friends! How cool is that?" Natalie gushes; she is officially fangirling.

"Earth to Natalie." I try my hardest to control my temper. "I really could use some help here!"

"I'd say wear something casual. You are the one who will be there for the whole day. I still don't know why you want to go for the whole day. You are going to be bored to tears in no time and if you dress too stuffy then you will be totally uncomfortable and look like you are trying too hard." She ends her spiel. "Not that you aren't going to stick out like a sore thumb as it is," she adds under her breath.

"What? Why would you say that?" I look at my reflection in the closet mirror.

"Because there are never men at her signings unless they are unlucky husbands." She giggles. "So…" She hesitates.

"Spit it out." I sift through the hangers of shirts in the closet.

"What made you decide to befriend her in the first place?" Natalie takes a deep breath. "Why are you pursuing her now?"

The answer is too simple. Her voice when we first did a take down together. She was on voicechat giving direction to the group. She was so sure of herself. Elsie's character Cybira is a commander in our clan. Her manner is stern but patient. It is amazing to hear her explain to new people how to play their character to get the most out of their experience. She has so much passion about the game and the people she associates within it. There is no way to convey all this to my sister. "I don't know. Talking to her just felt right." This is the answer I stick with. "And I want to know all there is to know."

"Are you going to ask her out?" Her tone is low; she is fishing for information.

"I don't know, maybe. I just wanted to know more about my friend, and I will see where that goes. Let's not make this more than what it is. That way if it doesn't pan out neither of us gets hurt." I tap the phone screen to check my time. I have fifty-two-minutes to get to the bookstore. "I will see you later."

Natalie sighs. "Okay, see you there later, Bradley." She disconnects.

I pull on a pair of khaki cargo pants and a light blue polo shirt. I feel my heartbeat speed up as I get closer to my front door to leave. I make quick work of the shoelaces on my Vans, grab my car keys, my phone, and my wallet before leaving for the Barnes and Noble. My mind spins as I open my front door to leave, and I double back to my bedroom to retrieve the little black box my mother sent me when I moved out here. A nagging thought between my brain and my heart keeps telling me this woman might be the one for me. If she is the same person online as she is in real life..

The building is only about a seventy-minute drive from my house. Parking is plentiful as no one in their right mind would be here this early for the signing. The workers are busy setting up the table and seating. A quick glance around I see that the Starbucks is in the middle to the far left of where I came in. Caffeine sounds heavenly right now. There is a woman in line ahead of me. She pays and quickly moves away leaving me to give my order.

"I'd like a medium coffee." I pull out my wallet to pay.

"The woman in front of you paid for yours, sir." The barista informs me. I turn to look for the woman who was in front of me just moments ago. No one is in the seating area.

"Mariah," I other barista calls loudly. A minute passes, and my cup is handed to me. I grab it and wait for the elusive pay it forward woman to come claim her coffee.

"Elizabeth," one of the barista's calls. I see two women come closer, deep in conversation as they grab their coffee. Before I can thank either woman, Mr. Antik bustles over.

"Ms. Williams, I am so glad you are doing this event today. If there is anything I can do please let me know." He holds out his hand to the women. My breath catches as Elsie looks up at the broad man and takes his hand. Her pictures don't do her justice. Her eyes are sharp light gray pools, and her dark hair is loose and skims her hips. Elsie is curvy, she fills out her jeans perfectly.

"Thank you for hosting this event. Is there anything I can do to help you set up?" She looks around the sales floor at the preparations underway. Her brow furrows as a look of concern overtakes her face. "Are you anticipating a large gathering?"

Mr. Antik ushers the two women away from me. The small trio disappears amongst the shelves. I sit at a corner table in the seating area, glad in my decision to come so early. A few minutes later the women come back to the small café area and sit at the table in front of me.

Elsie takes the seat furthest from me, but she is facing me so I can see her face, and the other women is in line for a few moments before she takes the seat next to Elsie.

"I know you hate technology, Elizabeth, but you really need to be careful." The woman takes a sip of her hot drink.

Elsie rolls her eyes but gives her companion a warm smile. "I just don't see the harm in talking to someone on the phone." She plays with the receipt sticker on her drink. "I don't hate technology. I just don't see the point in posting every moment of my life for strangers to read and comment on."

"And talking to a complete stranger that calls your number out of the blue is better? Are you that hard up for a friend?" The other woman stands up to pick up the food she had ordered a minute ago.

"Mariah! She was a lonely woman living in a nursing home hundreds of miles away, she was missing her child. Who am I to not have time for someone who just wants someone to listen to her?"

"How do you know she isn't a reporter or something!" Mariah's tone is full of anger, but she keeps her voice low.

"I don't know that. And to be frank, I don't care. It isn't like I told her anything that anyone couldn't find online about me."

"You told her your actual name, not your nickname," Mariah whispers.

"Okay, if that is the beginning of my downfall, I accept my fate." Elsie takes a pinch of the coffee cake in the middle of the table.

Mariah shakes her head and gives Elsie a sad smile. "I'm worried about you."

Elsie nods. "I know you are." She reaches over to squeeze her companion's hand. "Mariah, I wish you could accept the fact that I am perfectly happy how I am. I see how happy you and Nate are and my heart is content knowing you are taken care of and happy."

Mariah opens her mouth, but Elsie interjects, "I know, I know. Twenty-nine isn't old. You still hold out hope I will find Prince Charming." Elsie gives a rueful smile, "My writing is not reflective of what I am looking for in this life."

"One day you will find—"

"I wish you wouldn't hold out such hope. I hate to be a disappointment to my only family."

"You need to let your guard down once in a while." Mariah lets out an exasperated sigh. "You can't get upset that I want my sister to be happy." A small silence fills the space as they both drink their coffees. Mariah puts her cup down then places her hand on top of Elsie's. "So, you wrangled me in to coming at this ungodly hour to this event, why? You never come this early to signings."

Elsie bows her head. "I have a feeling that today's event is going to be different."

Mariah moves her hand to Elsie's shoulder. "Everything will be okay. We can work on an outline or something in the meantime."

Elsie shakes her head. "I am going shopping."

"Why? You are here for the next couple of days, save shopping for another day."

"Are you trying to curb my excursion into civilization?" Elsie laughs, the sound is pure magic. My stomach is instantly full of butterflies. "I really like the house I rented."

"Oh? Are you thinking of buying something out here and getting out of Ohio?"

"I can hear the hope in your voice. Do you want to move out

here?" Elsie poses the question, "How would Nate feel about relocating so far from his parents?"

"I have my ways of convincing him." Mariah laughs, before taking another drink.

"You can work from anywhere, Mariah. You don't need to stay in Ohio for me." Elsie tucks her hair behind her ear with one hand while the other brings the cup to her lips.

"What if you finally let that nice friend online get to know you and he wants you to move closer to the head of whatever that game is called."

"*Annex.*" Elsie rolls her eyes as she corrects her sister. "Headquarters are actually close to here, only thirty minutes or so away."

"Not everyone in California is your enemy, Elizabeth." Mariah's tone is playful, but her gaze is sharp.

CHAPTER 12

*E*LSIE

"On that note, I need you to put a copy of Height of Happiness at the front desk with the name Mizbahavin on it. I also need you to make sure everyone who asks a question writes it on the card to hand to you before they ask it."

"I still don't get why you have fans do that."

"I like to go back and read them and see if my answers have changed. If I have grown since that question was asked." I give her a smile.

"You're still an odd one, dear Elizabeth." Mariah shakes her head and tucks a lock of blonde hair behind her ear. "Okay, so we have hours to kill, where are you wanting to shop?"

I take my time to look around us. "Well, since I am going to be writing a new series, I need to look for a new journal. I also would like to look at a few new releases I have put off reading."

Mariah sighs. "Where do you find time for your life?" She studies me. "You aren't sleeping again, are you?"

"I'm fine. I can sleep when I'm dead. Besides, I went to bed insanely early last night. I made up all the time I have missed lately."

"You'd have more time if you stopped playing that stupid

game so much, oh my God you might even find time to go on a date."

I roll my eyes. "I've gone on dates. Loads of them."

"In real life?" She challenges.

"Ouch." I clutch my heart, "Why do you wound me? You don't try to spare my feelings, do you?"

"Would you want me to?" Her right eyebrow raises at me.

I sigh. "No. I wouldn't hold back being honest with you. I expect you to be honest with me." I drink the rest of my coffee in silence. My mind taking in all the details around us. The conversation of the workers around us. The banter, the flirting, the heavy stare from the handsome stranger at the table in front of me. I commit as much as I can to memory.

"Come on, let's go get you a journal so that you can stop trying to memorize everything in this building." Mariah laughs, she holds out her hand to me as she stands.

I swat it away playfully. "I'm not that old yet!" Mariah glances at the man who has been watching us this whole time and looks back at me. A mischievous smile comes over her. With great flourish she drops to one knee in front of my chair that I am still seated in. My face flames. She loves to make a mockery of my habits.

"My dearest Emma, if I loved you less, I might be able to talk about it more." She pulls out my fake wedding set I got from Walmart, the one I insist on wearing when I am out in public.

I roll my eyes and take my rings from her. "You make a horrible Mr. Knightley." I laugh as we both stand.

"One day I will perfect the Darcy proposal." Mariah hooks her arm around mine as she steers us to the trash cans to throw away our cups. She turns to look at me before we set off out of the café area, "I have a fan question!"

I look at the ceiling. "Of course you do."

"I lie! I have two!" She bites her lip before speaking, "Which Austen man is your favorite? And have you ever written the perfect proposal in one of your books?"

"My favorite Austen man?" I scan the café and lose myself to the recesses of my mind. I search every Austen character I can think of and find there is no way to answer her in one easy word.

"Oh no, I have struck a vein." She crosses her arms. "I demand to hear this out. I refuse to shop with you until you explain the complexity on your face!" She turns me and directs me back into the seat I just vacated.

"You are so annoying." My tone is sharp but light. "How have you never read any of the most perfect books in the world?"

"I have a different favorite author." She winks at me.

"I think my favorite Austen man is a mix of four. I love the purity that is Edward Ferrars, in his love of Elinor. And I identify with her as well because she is content in life knowing she can't be with who her heart loves."

"That does not sound like a romance story," Mariah interjects.

"Everything works out for them but for most of the book you think it won't. The second, I love the power, steadfast, and humble way of Mr. Darcy. He realizes his faults, owns them, and then changes them to better himself. Not to get the girl. He doesn't think he has any chance of gaining her favor. Third, I adore Mr. Bennett. He is funny and sharp. He lives with his poor choice of wife, but he loves his daughters more than life. Lastly, Mr. Knightley." I sigh as I close my eyes with a smile. I open them again to shake my head at my only friend. "Mr. Knightley falls in love with his best friend. He is in the middle before he even knew it began."

"What if you could have any of them?" Her amber eyes sparkle as she listens to my every word.

"That is what the crux of romance stories is." I reach out and tuck her hair behind her ear, "Mariah, we sell the dream. But that is all it is." I give her a small smile. "A dream. A very common dream for women." I focus on her face for a second, leaning close to her I lower my voice to a whisper, "I will tell you my darkest secret because you are my chosen family, I am no exception to that dream."

Mariah smiles broadly. "I knew it! Have you ever written your perfect proposal?"

I scoff and stand up. "With or without you I am going shopping." Mariah types something in her phone before she gets up. Her expression on her face expectant as she stays rooted to the spot next to me. I sigh, "no, I have not written my perfect proposal, Mariah."

"I want to read your perfect proposal. Do you promise to write it into your next book?" I roll my eyes before I nod at her. She looks back at her phone. "You will have to fend for yourself for a little while. I have to meet Nate on his break." The information catches me off guard. It takes me a moment to cover my disappointment with understanding instead.

CHAPTER 13

$\mathcal{B}$RADLEY

I see the sadness overcome Elsie. Before she turns to look at her friend, she puts a smile on her face. "Of course, I'm a big tough girl, I can take care of myself." She playfully pushes Mariah's shoulder. "I can even tie my own shoes and everything."

"Do you even own shoes that have shoelaces?" Her question has them both laughing.

I watch as they successfully leave the café area. I shoot a text off to my sister.

$\mathcal{I}$ watch as they successfully leave the café area. I shoot a text off to my sister. Coming early has paid off.

Her reply is quick. No way! She's already there? Now what?

I'm at a loss on my next move. No idea. Throw me a bone, what should I do?

Is she alone? I stare at the text. Why would that matter?

Not yet. I hit send and look around to try and see the women who left before me.

My phone vibrates. What does that even mean? I smile, I can almost hear her annoyed tone in the text.

She has an assistant or something with her but she is leaving soon. I walk a bookshelf over from the café to try and find Elsie.

I really have no ideas for you, I'm a horrible sister.

I'll think of something. See you later? I start to put my phone in my pocket when I remember I hadn't told Natalie where her book was I borrowed. As I start to text her where I left it her text comes through.

Yes! I'm so excited

Your book is in my top right desk drawer she didn't get me one second to close out of the app before she text me back THX

I roll my eyes at her last text. I hate when she abbreviates. I'm convinced she does it just to annoy me. Out of the corner of my eye I see Elsie is walking toward the back of the store while Mariah walks out the glass double doors in the front. Without another thought I get up from the table and follow her. Careful to keep my distance and not make myself known. I watch as she moves from one bookcase to the next reading a few titles softly out loud. She pulls out a title here and there to look at their cover. She doesn't bother reading the back for most of them, just looks at the cover. She replaces them on the shelves when she is done inspecting. Elsie makes her way through the romance section quickly, then heads to young adult. She reads the titles softly again, but she doesn't pull any out to inspect, instead she pulls them out to gather in her arms.

"Ms. Williams, would you like me to take these to the front desk for you?" Mr. Antik pops up next to Elsie, and the woman makes a quick step back away from him. Her eyes full of fear, she blinks twice and recovers composure.

"You scared me." Elsie gives a small smile. "Yes, if you could hold these for me. I will collect them when the event is over."

The broad man holds out his hands. "Wouldn't it be simpler to get these in an eBook format? With all your traveling and work?"

She finishes handing him the six books she has collected so far,

"It would be, but it wouldn't be as supportive to my fellow authors." She looks at the shelf again, pulls another book out, and adds it to his stack. "And I prefer the real deal." She winks, "Thank you for the help, Mr. Antik."

"No problem, please, call me, Jeff." He offers a smile that is too warm. Is he flirting with her?

"Thank you." Elsie turns to move to the next aisle, effectively dismissing the man altogether. I feel a sense of pride in her rebuff. In that same moment I am worried that she will rebuff me if I ever try to get to know her. My heart sinks a little.

I hear her reading off titles softly again, this time she is in the fantasy section. Standing in front of the books I wrote for *Annex*. My entire empire is because I took my stories and made it into the most immersive online game in the world. I do not make a ton of money from the books, but I write them for myself mainly.

Elsie pulls out her phone and places it to her ear, "Hey, Mariah..." She waits a moment. "Quick question, did my preorder for the latest *Annex* book come already?" She puts her phone on speaker as she pulls out book seven and looks at the cover.

"Does it matter?" Mariah asks, she sounds exasperated.

"Of course, it does."

There is a pause, "You are asking this because you can't remember if you already read it aren't you?"

"Maybe..." Elsie scowls at her phone.

"You know they make an app that tracks the books you have read! It is not called Pester Mariah, funny enough."

"But then you would miss the opportunity to point out yet another short coming in my character and a part of your soul would starve and die," she teases.

Mariah lets out a sigh in frustration. "Just buy it again and reread it."

Elsie doesn't say anything. She just keeps looking at the cover.

"You already have twenty books at the front desk you want to read while you are here, don't you?"

Elsie gives her phone a disapproving look before hitting end. Ouch. Her phone starts to ring, it is the opening music to *Annex*. It makes my heartbeat faster. Elsie answers and puts it on speaker again.

"Love you, Water Sister," Mariah coerces.

Again, Elsie is quiet.

"You have to finish it! You can't hang up on me without saying it! We promised. Sisters by choice," Mariah pleads in a quiet earnest voice.

Elsie sighs. "Like blood." With that the phone disconnects, she puts it in her back pocket and resumes looking for books.

Elsie moves down the aisle and stops at the Death Burns Within series and my stomach churns. I grit my teeth as I see her touch each book on the shelf. She pulls out the newest one and opens the front cover to read the inside dust jacket. I am still an aisle over from her, I pull out a book in front of me and turn it over like I am reading it. A tall muscular man walks towards Elsie. Her back is to him, he gets a wide smile on his face, as he comes up behind her to wrap his arms around her.

"Roland! Leave Elsie alone, you are going to give her a heart attack and then you will be out of a job!" A tall, thin brunette shakes her head as she comes up next to Elsie. "I can't take him anywhere!" The man releases Elsie.

She turns toward them with a smile. "My quota for getting hugged by a sexy man has now officially been met for this month."

"Sorry, not sorry. I love giving hugs."

"I know. It is an asset at my signings to have such a personable cover model with me. The fans tend to go for you over me." Elsie laughs. "So, I should really thank you and take it as part of the deal in having you along."

"That's the spirit." The other woman laughs.

"Why are y'all here? I know you aren't coming to this *Q AND A*." Elsie tips her head slightly to peer at them.

"We just got into town and knew you would be here. We are

going to the con tomorrow. For funsies." Roland reaches out to take the book from her hand. "I don't read the kind of stories you write, so what would you recommend a fantasy reader?"

"Well, there is Death Burns Within or there are the *Annex* books at the other end. Both are perfection." Elsie watches as Roland pulls another Death Burns Within off the shelf. "Truly, grab the first in both series and decide which one you like better," she reasons.

"Which do you prefer? Gun to your head, have to answer one." He peers down at her.

"I would probably tell you *Annex*, but that is because you can see the world and interact with it if you really enjoy the storyline."

"Is that the game you are always playing whenever we call you?" The woman walks to the end of the aisle and pulls off a couple of the *Annex* books from the shelf.

"Yea, I love the different writing styles both series offer. *Annex* is written more as a history book, full of facts and lore, but Death Burns Within is written in first person and alternates who is talking. Both of the authors are different but amazing." Elsie takes time to observe the two picking which series to invest in.

"Excuse me, could my husband and I trouble you for an opinion," the brunette calls over, and I turn my head more to fully look at her. Her makeup is flawless, her hair neat, and her dress fits her perfectly. Without looking I place the book back on the shelf, and smile as I make my way over to the small group.

"Of course, how can I be of service?" I keep eye contact with the woman not trusting myself to look at Elsie.

"Have you read any of these books?" The woman holds out one book in each of her hands to me.

"I have only read the first book in that series." I point to Death Burns Within and offer her a smile. "But my honest opinion is that Death Burns Within is a story whereas *Annex* is a masterpiece."

"Thank you for your candor." She places the *Annex* book in her husband's hands and puts the other back on the shelf. "We will see you at the con. Roland has to feed and water me now." With a giggle she pulls her husband with her to the registers not waiting for a goodbye from anyone.

I move my gaze to look at Elsie. Her smile is soft, but her eyes aren't looking at me, she's fixated on something behind my shoulder. I hear him before I see him. "Miss Elsie, I know you have a few hours until your event, but I was wondering if you would like one of my associates to pick up some lunch for you." Mr. Antik's voice is smooth as he moves to stand next to me. He ignores me as he reaches out to run his fingers down her arm, in response Elsie crosses her arms and takes a step back.

"No, there is no need for that. My assistant will be back soon. She and I will head out for some lunch." Her voice is clear and to the point.

The man is not taking the hint. "I would be honored if I could take you out for lunch, or even dinner tonight." He steps closer, "I could take you..."

My decision is made as he keeps crowding her. "I would appreciate it if you would back away from my fiancé." It takes me two steps to put myself between the manager and Elsie. He looks up at me in surprise.

"I didn't read anywhere that Miss Elsie was engaged," he challenges.

"Show him your ring, honey." I keep looking forward, not taking my eyes off this repulsive human, shielding this woman from unwanted advances. I'm not convinced she will play along, but after a moment her hands come around my stomach in a sweet hug from behind me. She rests her head on my shoulder blade, and her hands are pressed palm down on my chest. My heartbeat is heavier with her touching me with so much reverence. The man looks at the hands on my chest. The wedding set Mariah gave her glitters in the store lights.

"I apologize if I offended either of you. I was not aware." He takes a tentative step back from us. Then another, and another. He finally turns around and makes his way away from us.

I take one of Elsie's hands in my own as I turn around to face her. As her gaze lifts to mine I bring her hand to my lips and kiss it. "Pleased to meet you."

She searches my face, finally she speaks, "I'm Elsie Williams. Thank you for stepping in just now." She doesn't try to move her hand, but she does shift her feet a little. Almost like a little dance to keep herself from running away. "I normally have Mariah with me to prevent things like that from happening." She looks away from me and continues, "Things are so different now." She smiles and looks back up at me. "But that's the way of the world isn't it? Always changing, even if we don't want it to." She moves her hand out of my grasp. "You're the man from the café area earlier."

"Sorry, I remembered your friend had made a show of giving you a ring and I used that. I should have thought that through a little more." I tread carefully, I'm not sure how she will react.

She laughs, it is clear and pure. It is now my most favorite sound in the world. "I'm so grateful you stepped in. I tend to get overwhelmed when I am left alone."

I nod. "I can't imagine." I take a step back to give her space. "Would you like to find a place to sit and talk?"

"Um..." She looks around then back at me. "Yes, please. I would like that very much."

"Shall we?" I offer my arm to her and she doesn't hesitate to take it. We walk in sync with confidence back to the café area.

"Please. So, what should I call you?" she asks as I pull out a chair for her to sit.

"What would you like?" I turn my gaze to the menu trying to buy myself a little more time, effectively dodging the question for another moment.

"Hmm, I think I will have another iced coffee, please. I'm not very hungry yet."

I take a moment to place our order and pay. I sit across from her and finally give myself permission to look at her.

"So." She tilts her head a little, a lock of her dark hair falls over her eye. "What is your name?" She takes a moment to tuck her hair behind her ear and fold her hands in front of her.

"Are you really Elsie Williams?" I challenge her with a smile on my face and butterflies in my stomach.

She smiles and laughs. "Of course, why would I lie about that?"

CHAPTER 14

*E*LSIE

The man sitting in front of me is unassuming and nonthreatening, but I know from when I had my hands on his chest that he is solid. He is over six foot two. His eyes are cerulean. He is dressed in khaki cargo pants and a blue polo. His cologne is spicy and clean. His dark hair has a couple of silvered hairs sprinkled within it. I mentally shake myself to bring my attention back to the man in question.

"My sister is one of your biggest fans. I am meeting her here later for your signing."

I feel heat creep up and flood my face. His baritone is soothing. I feel like I have heard it before. I search my memory.

"Wait." I breathe. "I know you."

He smiles at me. To any other female it might be described as panty dropping, but I'm not looking for a romantic complication. "Do you?" His tone is laced with hope.

"Thorantik." I sit back in my chair and stare at the man.

"I prefer to be called Bradley." He leans forward to rest his arms on the table.

"So, who calls you Derrik?" I put my elbow on the table and lean my head on my hand as I stare at the man I have been talking

65

to for over two years online. Now I have a face to go with the man, for once my imagination did not serve me well.

"My employees, acquaintances, and generally anyone not my family." He pauses, his tone now a whisper. "Are you disappointed?"

I take my time to look at him. To take each of his features into account. To commit them to my memory. He allows me to take my time. Finally, I feel confident to answer him. "I am pleasantly surprised." I allow a smile to overcome me. "I am flattered your sister even knows me."

Before either of us can say anything, the barista calls his name, as our order is ready. He swiftly moves to go collect it and return. His demeanor is changed. He seems more on guard.

"Are you disappointed?" My anxiety gets the better of me and the question breaks the silence between us. His actions slow as he divides up the order between us. He is buying time to answer.

His gaze locks on mine. "You are stunning." The heat from earlier doubles on my face. Before I can even think so say thank you for the compliment he continues, "Not just in person, but on paper too. I took time to read your first book."

He has taken time to actually read one of my books, my heart melts a little. I turn my attention to the muffin he had placed in front of me, the reason I need to avoid this man slams into the front of my mind. He is the owner and creator of *Annex*. There is no room for me in his life or him in mine.

"What are you thinking just now?"

"Nothing."

"Something made you sad. You must have thought of something painful. You can tell me anything, you know. I haven't held back much over the last twenty-four months." He smiles encouragingly.

I take a deep breath, steel my nerves, and tell him the truth. "There is no room in your life for me, and no room for you in mine." I shrug my shoulders in defeat. "Friendship is all either of us can afford right now in our professional lives."

BRADLEY

Her words hit right in my heart. She feels something too, or else she wouldn't have said that. "Are you willing to leave this unexplored?"

She picks at the muffin in front of her, on impulse I grab her free hand. "What if this could work, if we were both willing to give it a real chance."

Her gaze lifts from the muffin to mine. Her breathing is a little faster than usual. "Can I think about it? I don't know what you read about me, but I have never officially dated anyone. My writing is my entire life." Her voice is breathless.

"I am fine waiting for you to decide that you deserve to find happiness, even if it isn't with me. But I would be honored if you would go on a date with me." I give her a moment to absorb what I said. "I'd wait a lifetime to spend time with you." This is the most honest thing I have ever said to any woman.

Her blush is adorable. I like how quickly I can instigate one out of her. Her phone rings, again it makes my heart skip that her ringtone is something I created. "Hello?" she answers. She says nothing else. Her demeanor quickly changes from happy, to shocked, to apprehension. A few minutes pass before she speaks again. "Okay," she whispers before she hangs up the phone. The color has drained out of her face. Her expression is full of worry.

My own phone rings. I check the caller ID, Ashley Allen, my public relations manager. Instinctively I roll my eyes and answer it, "Yes?"

"You have made the front page of every social media outlet!"

"What are you on about?" I take a drink of my coffee.

"Apparently you have become engaged to the author Elsie Williams." I choke on my drink as I start to laugh. "That is newsworthy?"

"Is that a trick question?" Her voice is calm.

"I might have told someone that." My eyes are weary as I watch Elsie. She is playing with her hair and avoiding my gaze. I reach out to grab hold of her hand as I keep talking. "What would you suggest I do?"

"This is good for publicity, so if you can keep up the rouse then go for it. Unless you are really with her…"

"Would it be a bad thing if I were?"

"No. Then I would offer you congratulations and wish you both happiness."

"There is no comment from us at this point, it is no one's business at this time," I instruct and hang up.

"Was that your PR?" Elsie whispers.

I nod. "She wished us happiness."

Elsie moves to take her hand back from me, but I move to lace my fingers with hers. "It's okay, everything will be fine." She stops trying to get away. After a moment she bows her head.

"Okay, I will go on a date with you." She raises her head, a sweet smile on her face. I smile back. I feel like I just won the biggest prize in the world. "Would you like to finish my shopping with me?" Her question melts my heart.

"That sounds perfect." We finish our muffins and coffee in happy silence. Elsie gathers our trash. We stand at the same time; she walks to throw away the trash and I stand by the entrance to wait for her. "This doesn't count as our date."

"You know, you can just be yourself. You don't have to be something you aren't." She gives a soft laugh.

I clutch my heart and stagger with as much drama as I can muster. "You wound me. How do you know I am not this doting and accommodating to everyone I am interested in?"

She stops laughing. "You're right, I don't." She places her arm through mine, as if it were second nature already, I feel sated in this moment. "But please, know, if we are exploring this idea then it needs to be genuine. I don't want to play games." She looks up at me. "If it comes a time where you don't want to do this anymore, just tell me."

"Why would you think I wouldn't be honest about something so serious?" I keep my voice low as I place my hand over hers on my arm.

"I just don't want to play games or waste time. If we don't fit than it's better to cut ties and go back to being online friends only."

"Ouch." I suck in a breath, loudly through my teeth like I was burned. "Trying to friendzone me already?"

"The jury is still out." She leads us back to the fantasy aisle. "So, you are the owner and creator of *Annex*." She removes her arm from mine as she looks at the long shelf in front of us. "What does that actually entail?" She pulls out one of the *Annex* series and caresses my embossed name on the cover.

I stare at her. "I'm not sure I understand your question." With a deep breath I nod. "Yes, I have been the sole writer for it since it began. Six years ago my brother, Shane, graduated college, and we decided to make the series into an online game. The rest is history." I smile at her. It is so freeing to be able to talk about these things. She doesn't care who I am, she is taking all of this in stride because on some level she is my equal.

She puts the *Annex* series back and moves to pick up a Death Burns Within book. I'm not going to lie, that kind of hurts. "Have you read the *Annex* series?"

She looks up at me. "Mariah got them for me a few years ago.

I didn't know about the series. I have been playing the game for five years. I was part of the beta launch."

Stick a fork in me. She is perfect. I can't help falling for this woman. But her holding onto that other series is slowly killing me. She gives me an odd look and looks down at the book in her hand. She pulls it closer to her heart. "Have you read this series?"

"I read the first one then stopped. I have read reviews, my sister's ex-boyfriend used to read them. So, he would tell me what they were about." I shrug. "I just feel like they are a cheap knockoff of *Annex*, so I don't bother with them."

Her perfect brow furrows in confusion. "You have such conviction over a series you have never read?"

"From what I have been told about them, yea. I also would not want to read something that might hinder my ability to write my own authentic storyline."

"I need to call Mariah and give her a heads up on 'us'." She pulls her phone out of her back pocket. A couple of taps and the screen and the light sound of ringing starts.

"Do you want some privacy?"

She shakes her head. "Hey, where are you guys?" She smiles and rolls her eyes as she trails her fingers over the spines of the books on the middle shelf of books. "Um, so, Laura called me." Elsie pulls a book off the shelf and reads the back at the same time she is talking. "So, *Annex*." I hear the other woman on the other end speaking but I can't make it out. "No, I am not asking you to bring my laptop. I'm trying to tell you something about *Annex*." Pause. "So, remember I have a special friend in the game that I have been talking to for a while." More talk I can't make out. "About two years?" Elsie puts the book back on the shelf, but doesn't push it all the way back in, she picks up another at the end of the same shelf. Again, she reads it as she speaks to her friend, "So, he's here." She laughs, "Yes, a real HE." Another eyeroll. "Well, the manager of the store came on to me after you left me. He was persistent and didn't want to take no for an answer." Raised voice coming from the other side of the phone, "That is what I am trying to tell you. My special friend stepped in and saved me." She replaces that book and again doesn't push it all the way back. "He told the manager I was his fiancé." Shrieking. Mariah is so loud Elsie pulls the phone away from her ear, at the same time she pulls another book off the next shelf. "So, apparently it is all over social media that I am now engaged." This time she puts the book back correctly. "So, Laura wants us to keep it up to stir up more publicity." She giggles. "Yes." Elsie looks at me, "I'm not sure. Maybe?" She gives a frustrated sigh as she turns her attention back to the books on the shelf. "See you then." She pauses. "Like blood." She hangs up.

With care I walk closer to her. "She okay with this?" I watch as Elsie collects the books on the shelf she didn't push all the way back.

"She is getting married on Saturday, so she wants everyone to be as in love as she is." Her sigh could mean almost anything. "Mariah is the biological daughter of the last foster family I lived with before I turned eighteen. She is the sister I would have chosen if I had the choice." The sentiment of water sister and like blood come to my mind.

"Is that why you end your calls with water and blood?"

She nods. "Blood is thicker than water, but you need water to survive this life. I love her as if she were my blood relative." She looks up at me "Other than you, she is my only friend."

"But you will gain a brother when she gets married," I encourage. Elsie smiles but it doesn't reach her eyes. "Tell me what you're thinking."

"I need you to only call me 'Elizabeth' when we are around her and Nate. He doesn't know that Mariah works for me, or what I do." She hesitates, "Do you promise not to judge me too harshly?"

I make a gesture to cross my fingers over my heart and kiss them. She giggles. "Mariah will make her own family. That does not include me. She will have Nate and one day kids." She pauses as we move back to the romance section. "With all my heart I am happy for her. He is her perfect match." She reaches on to the shelf and pulls out a book. We are at the bookshelf of her works. It spans several shelves. The book she is looking at is titled *Finding My Forever*. "I know. I already wrote their story."

I take the book from her. "What do you mean?" I read the back. It is a story of Mariah and Nate finding their missing pieces in each other and finding complete happiness, according to the back. I put the book back on the shelf. I look at the other titles. "You write based on real couples?"

She gives me a small smile. "Sometimes." Elsie looks back at her books. "A good amount are just wishes or dreams women have for their futures."

"Are any of them based on your wishes or dreams?"

CHAPTER 16

*E*LSIE

Hearing him say that my pride and joy, the one writing that has ever meant anything to me, is a "cheap knockoff" hits my heart hard. I could tell him that I wrote my books and copyrighted them over a decade ago. I could tell him that my series is absolutely nothing like his, but my heart hurts too much right now. I remind myself this is just two people who enjoy each other's company, and we aren't in a deep relationship. There is no need to reveal this part about myself.

Can this man ask any more spot-on questions? "No." I look at this man who has taken the trouble to track me down. "My dreams aren't marketable to the masses."

He tilts his head a little to study me. "If I were to ask, would you tell me your dreams?"

My answer is quick and honest. "Maybe if we had been together for a substantial amount of time. One day I would probably feel compelled to tell you all of them."

"Fair enough." I think he attempts to assuage my anxiety and take the pressure off me. Without much thought I put my arm around his waist and pull him closer to me. I lean my head on his shoulder as we stand looking at my accomplishments. "I want you to know, I am proud of what you have done for yourself. Not that you need my adoration or compliments. I am; I'm proud of you."

"Thank you," I whisper. There is a slight pressure on my side, Bradley firmly settles his arm around my waist. My phone rings again. I pick it up without looking at the caller ID.

"Hello?" I do not move from Bradley's warmth.

"Yes, hello. I am calling on behalf of the Miller family." There is a pause, I wait for her to continue. "And I am looking for their daughter, Elizabeth Lucus."

"This is she, but I do not have family of the last name Miller." I feel a headache forming behind my eyes. This song and dance has been played before, and I am over it.

"Yes, ma'am, they told me you would probably have no idea who they are." I hear papers shuffling on her end of the phone. "They would like you to take a DNA test to establish your identity."

"Why would I do that? I have not gone gallivanting around looking for them, so why would I jump through such hoops? Do they assume I am a trained animal?" I fail to keep the disdain out of the tone.

"Not at all, I assure you. They merely want to provide proof to the estate to make sure you get your rightful inheritance."

"No, thank you." I don't wait for a response. I slip my phone back into my back pocket after I hang up on the woman. Bradley squeezes my body closer to his for a moment. Almost like a supportive side hug.

"Wanna talk about it?" His head is tilted towards the books on the shelf in front of him. His lips move wordlessly. He is reading my titles.

I appreciate the Adonis next to me, the man admiring my work. "Just another 'family' coming to claim me now." I use air quotes with my free hand, I am not ready to give up the feeling of his body next to me, the feel of his hard body under my hand.

"Oh?" He looks at me finally. His gaze is piercing and full of curiosity.

"Yes, every few months I seem to get a person emailing me about their DNA tests and their family history. This one sent a representative and wanted a DNA test to establish my connection."

"Why would they do that?"

"According to the person on the phone I am in line to get some sort of inheritance." I shrug.

"Money isn't a motivator for you?"

CHAPTER 17

BRADLEY

Everyone wants money. Especially those without it. I look Elsie up and down for the thousandth time. She is clearly down to earth and unassuming. She doesn't scream I have an exuberant amount of money.

She shakes her head. "I make my own money. I don't need someone to hand me any." She disengages from me to roam the aisles again.

I keep pace with her. "You aren't even a little curious?" I smile. "What if it was enough to fund the cure for cancer or something?"

She turns to look at me. I stop in front of her, worried I have overstepped myself. But as her eyes bore into mine. I get the sense she is trying to form her thoughts into words. So, I wait.

She bites her lower lip. "Money like that would come with more stipulations and strings than I would ever be comfortable working with." She grabs a small lock of her hair and starts to braid it. "Money like that is not free and is not earned by me."

"What if you one day fell in love with a man with an ungodly amount of money?" I give her my best smile.

77

She releases the lock of hair, and her lips part. I take the chance to brush my lips over hers. She doesn't respond to me so I start to pull away. Her fingers lace into my hair and her mouth opens. She is sweet and soft. Her tongue is tentative as it caresses mine. She pulls away slowly.

"I'm sorry." She doesn't move away. Her lips still close to mine. Her eyes are still closed. "I'm not sure what came over me." She opens her striking silver eyes, her face tilted up to mine.

"I'm not sorry." I trail my fingers down her cheek.

"Were you talking about you a moment ago?" she whispers, but all rational thought has left my head.

"When?" I nuzzle her nose with mine.

"The part about asking what I would do if I fell in love with someone with more money than sense." She smiles but it isn't happy. It has sadness in it. I nod. Not willing to risk saying anything. She takes a step away from me. The loss of heat is profound in the moment. She is worrying her bottom lip with her teeth. I give her space and time. I remember the letter she sent me in game.

"Money causes problems in even the most genuine relationships."

"That can be true." With all the caution I can muster, I carry on, "What if it wasn't a factor?"

Her gray eyes open wider. "But in this instance, it is a factor." She takes a step back to bring more space between us. "I am going to go to the dress store across the plaza."

"Do you want to be alone?"

She glances back to the exit toward her destination and then back to me. "You want to go shopping with me?"

"I have been doing it for a while and I enjoy spending time with you." I move to take her hand. "Plus, we are supposed to be selling this idea of a happy healthy couple."

Her mouth turns down into a small frown, her eyes dim a little, and she nods. "Of course." She lets me take her hand. "Is there anywhere you would like to go while we are out?"

"Maybe, if something catches my attention." Together we walk to the exit and head to the other shops nearby.

Her hand is small and warm in mine. It fits naturally. Our kiss is still replaying in my mind. I barely register that I am standing alone inside the entrance of a woman's clothing store. My hand grows colder with the loss of hers. I blink hard and look around for Elsie. I spot her a few racks of clothes in with her cell phone out.

"I'm shopping for clothes." She laughs easily. "You on your way back?" A pause. Her voice gets quieter, it takes more effort to hear her. "I also take back my harsh judgment of you and Nate kissing in public all the time. I thoroughly approve if the kisser is exceptional." I hear a raised voice on the other end of the phone, then Elsie, "It was one, and it might have been exactly how I wrote about it."

Whoa. Wait a minute. She spots me coming closer. "I'll see you in a bit." Her eyes lock on mine, "Like blood." She whispers and hangs up.

"Well, hello there." I give her a smile. "Are you single?"

Her brows knit in confusion, then relax, "No, haven't you heard? I am now the fiancé of some higher up at a little game company. But it is all for show, so..." She gives me a small smile. "I'm single."

Ouch. "So, this is all only for show?" I challenge her.

Her smile falters, she moves her weight from foot to foot, "Bradley..." I move to stand in front of her, my mouth silences her.

It is just a chaste kiss. "Didn't we just agree to give this a shot? Let our PR's give statements about an engagement to make all of them happy but in general, we really do give this a try?"

I pull away from her enough to look down at her. "I was perfectly honest in my message in game, and I am being upfront with you on the issue of having money." Her voice is soft, her eyes shyly averted.

"Every relationship has their issues. It is how we work through them that will determine if this is worth fighting for."

She tilts her head slightly, and her eyes sparkle as the light through the front windows of the store shines on her. "Okay."

CHAPTER 18

$\mathcal{E}$**LSIE**

What am I doing? Am I really going to agree to this hair-brained idea? I close my eyes to shut out the world around me. One deep breath. Two deep breaths. Three deep breaths. I open my eyes, half expecting to wake up in my bed and this all being a dream. Bradley's blue eyes are watching me with the utmost alertness. Movement behind him catches my attention. I see Mariah and Nate enter the store. "Remember to call me 'Elizabeth' in front of everyone. The only exception is when Mariah is alone with us." I look at Bradley to make sure he heard my whisper. I instantly relax as I see him nod.

"What is this? I leave you alone for literally three hours and you go and get yourself engaged?" Mariah's voice is full of mirth.

"I never do anything by the book, you know that."

"That's for sure." She comes to stand next to Bradley.

Bradley extends his hand out. "Hi, glad to meet you I'm Derrik."

I take note of how he introduces himself. We have that in common, and part of me wonders if he does it to hide a secret like I do or if it is just to make the distinction of proximity within the relationship. Do I get to call him Bradley because we have known each other for years, or maybe he lets me in the closer tier because we have commonality in our position in this life. My brain starts to hurt so I quickly resume introductions. "This is Mariah. Mariah, this is Derrik." I smile as they evaluate each other and shake hands.

"This is my fiancé, Nate." Mariah turns to loop her arm around her man's arm. The shaggy red haired man is only an inch or two shorter than Bradley. They smile at each other and shake hands.

"Pleasure to meet you both." Bradley's voice is velvet soft.

"So, when is the wedding?" Nate nudges my shoulder with his.

"Mariah agreed we could have a double wedding," I tease. Nate's eyes widen in shock. I roll mine. "Relax, I wouldn't do that to you."

Nate visually relaxes. "You'll never get married." He wipes his brow dramatically.

I can't help but chuckle despite the mocking tone of his voice. "Probably not." I shake my head and move back to look for a summer dress.

"Why are you in here anyway?" Mariah calls out. She sighs loudly. "You only brought one outfit, didn't you?"

"That is not true!" I turn towards the small group. "I brought plenty of outfits!"

"Elizabeth! I know at least half of those are your cosplay!" Mariah scolds.

"It's clothing!" I yell as I turn to look for my style.

"She cosplays?" I hear Bradley ask behind me.

I choose to ignore him. I'm sure he will grill them for more information on me and at this point it just saves me the trouble of talking about myself anymore. I gather several summer dresses with flared skirts and head to the dressing rooms.

CHAPTER 19

BRADLEY

We watch Elsie gather several dresses and head off to the back of the store.

"Is this thing you have goin' on just for revenue or..." Mariah's amber eyes are sharp as she stares hard at me.

"We are letting the PR people handle what is released to the public but for the sake of pulling hairs, we are dating." I rub the back of my neck. "I think. It has been a battle to get her to agree to go on a date with me."

Nate burst out in a loud laugh. Mariah turns her sharp gaze on him. Nate quickly clears his throat and gives her a little grimace. "Sorry, baby." He softly clears his throat again. "I know she is special to you."

Mariah's eyes blaze. "She's my sister." Nate avoids her stare.

"But she isn't technically..." he starts.

"No, they are closer than sisters." I glance from Mariah to the back of the store where Elsie is. "It wouldn't surprise me if their bond didn't transcend time itself."

Mariah's jaw drops, her eyes brim with tears as she gapes at me.

83

"Are you okay?" I hear Elsie's voice coming closer to us, her arms full of dresses.

"Here let me hold those. I think Mariah needs a hug." I grab the pile from Elsie and drape them over my forearm as Elsie quickly envelops her only family.

"What's wrong?" she whispers, she glances at Nate who is still looking ashamed and then to me, "What did you do?"

Clearly, she is using the collective "you" since she doesn't know which of us upset her sister. I'm not willing to speak up since I am not exactly sure which of us offended her.

CHAPTER 20

Elsie

LSIE

Mariah is full on crying when I pull her to me to hug her. Her body is lightly shaking. Nate looks guilty and Bradley looks concerned and confused. "Do you wanna get some air?" I whisper to her. She nods, her grip on me tightens. I shuffle us outside. I pat her back softly as I let her cry her heart out.

"Elizabeth," she calls as her sobs slow. "That man." She draws in a raspy breath. "It is like he stepped out of the pages of a romance novel." Sobs start anew.

"What on earth are you talking about, Mariah?" I kiss the top of her head.

"Nate never understands our bond, but that man met me for all of two minutes and gets us."

"I've known him for a while. I talk about you all the time, of course he understands us." I chance a glance inside the store to see if I can see the man she is going on about. I don't see him where we left him and Nate. My heart breaks a little hearing the confirmation that Nate doesn't understand us. Does that mean he thinks I am their third wheel? Am I the third wheel in this relationship? Does he have plans to get Mariah away from me? My anxiety is threatening to take over, but I will myself to stay calm.

Mariah needs me right now. The men exit the store and walk with caution to us.

"Baby, let's go sit inside somewhere and get a drink and some air conditioning." Nate caresses Mariah's arm trying to coax her into his arms. After a moment Mariah relinquishes her hold on me and buries her face in Nate's chest.

"You okay?" I hear Bradley behind me. I'm too shocked by the turn of events to look away from Nate trying to corral Mariah into the chain restaurant on the corner of the strip. Bradley steps in front of me, he bends his knees so he can be eye level with me. "Elizabeth." His gaze holds worry in it, his voice is still strong, but softened with concern, "Honey, are you ok?"

My gaze snaps to his, and I shake my head to clear it. "I'm okay. What happened? I was only gone a couple of minutes!" It is then I realize he is holding several bags in his hands.

"I didn't know which ones you wanted, so I got them all." He maneuvers the bags onto one of his wrists, he wraps his free arm around me. His body is warm as it encircles me, his attempt to comfort me works in seconds.

"You didn't need to buy me anything." My voice is a whisper. Bradley's warmth calms my anxiety.

Bradley reaches up and tucks some of my hair behind my ear. "Mariah needed you and I didn't want to interrupt."

"Thank you for realizing she needed me."

"Want to follow them into the restaurant?"

I nod. Bradley pulls away but keeps his bagless arm around my waist as we walk together to the chain Chinese restaurant. Despite everything, I take note that the ease that we interacted online translates and bleeds over into how easy it is to be around and near him now.

"Hey!" Nate stands up from a round table in the corner of the dining area.

Bradley nods to him and steers us to the table. He pulls out my chair and places the many bags on the vacant seat on the other side of him.

"I'm sorry, Elizabeth." Mariah dabs at her eyes. "I had a moment."

"You never have to apologize to me," I whisper. I take my time to really look at my sister. She's an emotional mess. Her wedding is coming up and I know she is trying to make sure all the details are perfect. Maybe I should give her some time off from managing my life.

"Are you ready for the event?" Nate asks me, his smile is forced, his eyes are tight as he looks at Mariah and then me.

"Yea." I shrug. "It isn't like this is my first one."

"You've gone to twenty-two of these bookstore signings." Mariah smiles at me. It warms my heart to know she keeps track of literally everything in my life and also that she conceals my identity so easily. I know she keeps my job a secret to make things easier at home with her brothers, sometimes that hurts but it makes her life better for her. She also hasn't told Nate that I am Elsie Williams and that she manages my entire life, which I think is a huge mistake on her part. Keeping secrets is not a good way to start a marriage. I roll my eyes at myself, look who's talking. As I glance at Bradley, I wonder if he would care that I am the author of Death Burns Within. Maybe one day I will feel comfortable telling him my biggest secret.

"What can I get you all?" A tall, blonde man next to me asks, his voice interrupting my train of thought. His smile is genuine and inviting.

Bradley clears his throat and drapes his arm over the back of my chair. "What would you like, dear?"

I can't help but tilt my head at Bradley and consider the man. I contain the urge to roll my eyes. "I would like an iced tea and the won ton stir fry." I feel Bradley's fingers caress my shoulder.

"I will try the won ton stir fry as well, but I would like a Coke with mine." Bradley's voice is harder than usual.

"Is Pepsi okay?" The waiter asks.

Bradley looks at me. "Make mine an iced tea then." He gives me a slow smile.

"And we will have the spring rolls and some chicken fried rice. Please bring two plates." Nate orders for them both, "And she will have a water and I will have a Sam Adams."

"Bottle or draft?"

"Bottle, please." Nate collects our menus and hands them to the waiting server. He watches the waiter turn and leave before he looks at his fiancé. "Do you want to talk about it?"

Mariah still has her napkin held to her eyes dabbing at the tears that refuse to stop coming. She doesn't speak, more tears spring to her eyes.

"Sometimes, talking isn't needed." I keep my voice low.

"She's clearly upset." Nate's voice holds an edge of anger.

"She's sitting right here! Don't you think she would be talking if that is what she wanted to do?" I fail to keep my own anger in check. Not knowing what triggered this turn of events and seeing my sister so affected makes my skin feel too tight.

"Elizabeth, it's okay." Mariah puts her hand on mine. She turns to Nate. "Tonight, we need to have a talk."

Nate sits back in his seat. Defeat is written all over his face.

CHAPTER 21

*B*RADLEY

I see Elsie look from Mariah to Nate and back again. She is trying to figure out what is going on between her family. I hate that I can't help her. I am at a loss on it myself. I decide to try and move the conversation back to familiar territory.

"So, what exactly is a Q and A for romance authors?" I turn my full attention to the woman I am now in a relationship with. Part of my brain registers the humor in the entire situation I find myself in, but the rest of my brain is wholeheartedly enthusiastically excited for this change in circumstance.

"A small group of fans come and ask the author all sorts of questions." Her smile is quick. "I like the range of questions they ask." She gives a small laugh. "She once had a young fan ask her which Disney princess she identified with." Another giggle. "And her sister stood up and asked if she thought Gaston would beat Prince Hans in a fight to the death."

"Well?" I can't help but smile at her. "What did the author say?"

She eyes me seriously, and shakes her head. "You don't have to pretend to be interested in me."

My smile falters; I feel it slip; my heart hurts at her words. "If I didn't want to know, I wouldn't ask."

She studies me. Minutes tick by, and I hold her gaze. Our waiter appears with our food. Still, she keeps her eyes on me and remains silent. Our drinks are brought and finally Elsie looks away to put her straw in her drink.

"Of course, Gaston would defeat Hans," she says after she takes a drink of her tea. "And we both love the same princess, Giselle." She finally looks at me again. "It is the most underrated Disney movie of all time."

"I have never heard of Princess Giselle." I keep my face serious.

"We are giving this relationship a real try..." Elsie's voice is a whisper. "Right?"

I nod. I am totally enthralled with this woman.

"Then I will subject you to watching the best Disney movie of all time..." She gives me a devious grin, "Actually, I will torture you with watching all my favorite movies." She takes a bite of her food. she chews and takes a drink of her tea before finishing her devious plan. "To see if you stick around."

"Is that a challenge?"

Elsie's stare is sharp but before she can answer me Mariah interjects, "I have faith that Derrik will be not only a worthy opponent but that he might be in this for the long haul." Her voice is full of hope and encouragement.

I slyly wink at her. Nate clears his throat. "So, you guys are officially dating?"

Without missing a beat, I reply. "No, we are officially engaged." I correct.

Nate chokes on his bite of spring roll. Mariah rolls her eyes and pats him forcefully on the back. Her pats sound a little harder than necessary but that might be because she is still upset with him.

I take my chances and look at Elsie. I'm worried I said the wrong thing. She takes another small bite of food. I watch her chew and swallow. Her gaze lifts to mine, the world officially stops. She takes a cursory look around. Her movements are quick as she moves to place her lips on mine in a quick kiss. Just as quickly it happens, she goes back to finishing her food. As if affection and being with me were second nature. I take a bite and look at the shocked face of Nate and the approving face of Mariah. I feel I have an ally for life with that woman. We eat in easy silence until our plates are empty or close enough. I see the waiter make his way back to our table.

"Can I take your plates?" our enthusiastic waiter asks. I stack Elsie's plate under mine, and put the silverware on the top to hand for the man. "Thank you. Can I interest you in some dessert?"

"What do you have?" I ask as he takes Mariah and Nate's dishes.

"We have a chocolate volcano brownie and chocolate chip cookies a la mode." He looks at the women hopeful.

"Sure, bring us one of each but put the ice cream on a separate dish, please." I look at Elsie.

"You really have been talking for a while, haven't you?" Mariah cups her face and leans her elbow on the table to study us.

"I like to think I am good at retaining details when it comes to my friends and people who are interesting to me." I take a sip of my tea.

Our waiter brings us our desserts, extra plates, napkins, and utensils. He also brings fresh drinks for us all at the same time. He is a very attentive waiter. Nate seems annoyed by him.

Nate takes out his phone. "It is almost five now, should we think about heading back?"

I put two cookies on a plate and slide it to Elsie. I pull the ice cream closer to me and dip the spoon into it.

"Can I have a bite?" Elsie's voice is sweeter than any dessert I can imagine.

"Of course." I bring the spoon up to her waiting mouth. I remind myself not to gape at her swallowing ice cream. I take the spoon back and grab myself a bite. It isn't anything to write home about, but the vanilla is refreshing.

"Would you like to try some of mine?" Elsie smiles trying hard not to laugh.

"What is so funny?" I ask laughing at her attempt to hold in her own laughter.

"Because I almost asked if you wanted some of my cookie." She bursts into giggles and so does Mariah.

Taking the initiative, I lean over and take a bite of the cookie in her hand. "Mmmmm that is good. I have no idea what you find so funny." My words are garbled as I talk around my bite of cookie.

Mariah regains herself quicker. "Cookie is another word for vagina."

Everyone at the table laughs. Elsie who hadn't stopped laughing, laughs even harder. She wipes a tear from her eye. "Stop. I'm going to die." Elsie coughs as she laughs. She plays with the small computer on the table as she finishes her cookies.

We make quick work of the desserts. "I need to use the restroom," Elsie says as she stands. Mariah copies her and together they make their way to the other side of the restaurant.

A moment later the waiter brings us all to go cups of our drinks, except Nate. "Would you like a to go cup of a soda or some water?"

"No, thank you." Nate's tone is curt.

"I hope you all have a nice evening." He places four fortune cookies on the table then he turns and leaves our table.

"Where is the bill?" I ask Nate looking around the table.

"Elizabeth always pays when we go out." His tone is almost resentful. He gathers up the little cookie packages.

"You wish she didn't?" I ask as I put my straw into my to go cup and Elsie's into hers.

He rubs the back of his neck. "I love Mariah. She is my entire world." He sighs. "But her world is not just me."

I nod. "Not to totally play devil's advocate, but if you have kids one day will you feel like this toward your children?"

He lifts his head slowly to look at me. "That thought never crossed my mind, to be completely honest." He looks around for a moment. "Are you really into Elizabeth?" His tone is disbelieving.

His question catches me off guard, but I don't need to think of the answer. "We have been friends for a little over two years." I give him a small smile, "On impulse, I came to meet her today." I explain. "And I feel like my life might have actually started a few hours ago." I laugh. "Our relationship has always been easy and natural; it is even better in person." I stand up from the table. I grab the bags from the chair and our cups.

He shakes his head. "I have to tell you, before Mariah does," he spots them walking back to us, "if you hurt her, it will hurt my woman, and that I will never forgive. But I wouldn't blame you for deciding she isn't right for you." Nate watches with barely concealed annoyance as Elsie and Mariah make their way back to us.

I don't get a chance to answer him before the women are back to the table.

CHAPTER 22

$\mathcal{E}$LSIE

"Ready?" I smile up at Bradley as we come back to the table to collect the men. He offers me my to-go cup.

"Lead the way." He already has my bags in his other hand and his own cup, he offers me his free arm, which I gladly take.

"I will see you tonight when you roll in." Nate kisses Mariah on the cheek as he moves to cross the street away from the bookstore. "If you need me, text me." Nate disappears as we make our way closer to the bookstore.

"How does he not put two and two together and realize I am the author? Has he ever asked you why you have to attend every single event this author has?" I ask in disbelief at how oblivious Nate is.

"I told him from the first date that I am a huge Elsie Williams fan and no matter what I will be attending any event she has." Mariah shrugs. "He has never asked me to not go, and he is always happy when he gets to take time off to come with me."

We both laugh and shake our heads in unison.

We retrace our steps the short distance back to the bookstore, as soon as we round the corner apprehension laces through every inch of my soul, something is off. There are people all over outside. There seems to be some sort of line to get into the building. We wait our turn and quickly find refuge in the travel section. I look around, there are people with cameras you use for the evening news. The seating area I am used to having is standing room only with a little under an hour until the event. I don't realize how hard I am squeezing Bradley's hand.

"Elizabeth?" Mariah's voice is a whisper, but her urgency is as loud as an airhorn in my brain.

"Hey." Bradley keeps hold of my hand but steps in front of me, bending his knees so he can get eye level with me once again. "What do you need?"

Tears sting my eyes. "I need to breathe." I close my eyes and take a couple of deep breaths. "Mariah can you walk around as part of my promotional team and ask why there are cameras, and see if they are looking for someone else?" I open my eyes finally to look at her. She nods and quickly leaves to complete my request.

"Not a fan of crowds?" Bradley muses. I hear the slight strain in his voice.

"I'm fine with large crowds, when I can prepare myself for them." I take another deep breath.

Mariah rushes over. Her mouth set in a grim line. "They are here for you, Elizabeth." She reaches over to pat my shoulder with one of her hands. "They are following up on the story of you snagging one of the world's most eligible bachelors."

I groan. "See? This is why I don't do anything on social media." Mariah pats my shoulder some more.

"Silver lining," Bradley squeezes me tight, "I'm already here to help with those questions."

I look up at him. An idea starts to form in my mind. "I might have a game plan, but it is a big ask from me."

He tilts his head. "Hit me with it."

I swallow the anxiety that is threatening to erupt from my throat. "We could start a few minutes early and give them their moment to ask some questions and then let them go so my fans aren't overrun."

He blinks for a moment. "That is a really diplomatic plan." He smiles. "Let's do it."

I nod once and step towards the table I will be holding my *Q AND A*. I look at the clock on the back of the wall behind the row of cash registers, perfect I have thirty minutes before my event starts.

"Welcome, everyone. To my Q and A." I stand straight behind the chair I will be occupying for the next few hours. "I am Elsie Williams, and I am just so happy you all took time out of your day to come see me." I give myself a moment to collect my thoughts. "The event is scheduled to start in the next thirty minutes and my friends know how much I love to be exactly on time; I thought I would do a quick-fire Q and A with these fine people so they can hopefully get home at a reasonable hour."

With that Mariah steps up. "If you would wait until I call on you before asking any questions, we would be most appreciative." She looks around the room. "Before this gets out of hand quickly, we ask that only the reporters ask questions at this time and then please exit safely after this session. Also, since most of you are not fans and are new to who this is, this woman is Elsie Williams. She writes the Kismet Summers series. I am her personal assistant. If you have any questions you are welcome to email me in the future."

With that, hands immediately shoot into the air from all sides of the sea of people before me. Mariah picks a woman in a bubble gum pink tea length dress. "I am writing from the *Sun Times*, is it true you are only getting married because you claim you are pregnant?"

I can't help but laugh. "I assure you; I know for a fact that I am not pregnant. We simply grew to love each other over the last few years and now marriage is the next logical step for our relationship."

"You, sir." Mariah points to an older man toward the middle of this group.

"Some are claiming this is a result of a company take over, that you have been planted to gather evidence against Derrikson Entertainment. In order to effectively place a sort of gag order on you, and you are being blackmailed into this marriage."

I pinch the bridge of my nose. "Let's say any of that sounds even remotely sane, how on earth do you expect me to answer in the affirmative and not expose the scheme for what it is and jeopardize my own life?" I can't contain my eye roll. "No, that is completely false and bordering on total insanity. I suggest if that is the angle your boss went and had you stand here and waste your time, perhaps the owners of the company you represent should cut off any contact with Lifetime movies for their writers." I offer him a small sympathetic smile. "I am truly sorry, your company wasted your evening."

Bradley is standing off to the side, waiting for any question I might not be able to handle. I take comfort in that knowledge. The next question comes at me from left field, an average looking young woman asks, "Is the prenup for your upcoming marriage ironclad against you acquiring any stock of *Annex*?"

I see Bradley take steps to stand next to me, but I answer anyway, "Is that really any of your business?" Bradley beams at me. There is an audible gasp from the crowd.

"Good evening. I am Derrik Derrikson. I want to echo my fiancé's answer. That is no one's business." He places his arm around my waist.

The woman moves to reclaim her seat, "What makes you think there is a prenup or that if there is one that it wouldn't protect my own interests in my own empire?"

There are murmurs. Another woman stands up, "No offense, but how much could a small-town author make yearly in reality?"

I smile at her, "Sometimes, money is worthless, but reputation is everything."

Mariah moves to stand next to me, "Are there any other questions?" She scans the room, one man stands up, "Yes, Sir?"

"When is the wedding?"

I blank. I didn't expect them to go for the kill after just hearing of the announcement.

"We have not yet made that decision yet." Bradley squeezes me to him.

"One more question if I may, Miss Elizabeth." The man's tone is cold, like he knows more than he sees.

"I prefer to be called Elsie." I can't manage a smile this time, something about this man is off.

"May we see the engagement ring?" I furrow my brow, before I can move my hand Bradley grabs it and holds it tight.

"It is at the jewelers getting resized, so she is wearing a substitution for now." Bradley pulls my hand up to his lips and kisses the back of my hand before extending my hand out to show the crowd.

The man looks annoyed to be thwarted. He takes some notes and gets up with the rest of the press to exit the building. I take a deep breath. Now the fans who were standing can take a seat.

"Would you like me to grab you a bottle of water before you start talking?" Mariah asks. I nod my head at her. Mariah smiles and goes to complete her task.

"I would be honored if you would let me introduce you to my sister." Bradley looks down at me, as he waits for my answer.

"I would be grateful if you introduced her to me." I smile.

CHAPTER 23

BRADLEY

"Not to invoke my fiancé rights but would it be okay if my sister stands back here with me while you do your event tonight?" I give her my best smile as I try to curry favor.

Elsie giggles. "Sure, I will make sure Mariah has a couple of chairs put back here."

"We can stand," I insist.

"You will thank me for the chairs if you decide to stay the whole time." She sounds confident.

I look out over the crowed. I don't see my sister, but there are so many people in this cramped space that I decide to stop wasting time and hit the speed dial on my phone.

"Hello?" She is definitely in the line to get in, there is a ton of noise wherever she is.

"Hey, when you get in the doors meet me by the travel section," I instruct.

"Okay." She hangs up. From my vantage point by the books showing all the places to go to in Germany I watch Elsie get her space set up for what is to come. Mariah pulls out a box of permanent markers and Elsie arranges a couple of packs of post it note pads. The women work silently to make a cohesive assembly line.

Elsie hands a stack of index cards to Mariah. Mariah hands Elsie a bottle of water a drop of condensation drips from it as she grab it from her.

"Hey!" There is a light pressure on my arm, I turn toward the voice, Natalie is at my side. She looks a little flushed.

"You okay?" I ask.

"Yea, it is just a little more crowded than usual." She looks around us.

"Hey! Elsie said you needed a couple of chairs." Mariah drags two chairs behind her. "While I have a second can I please say something?"

I search her face for only a second. "Of course."

"Elizabeth is not only my best friend in the whole world, but she is also my chosen sister. I'm sure she has told you this. We have been each other's ride or die for over twelve years." She takes a deep breath. "I am ecstatic that these chips have fallen like they have. I know you are both going to give this a legit go." She looks over at Elsie who happens to have her back to us. "Don't give up on her. She has trust issues from never having anyone," she smiles, "Except for me of course." Her smile fades. "I'm serious. Elizabeth is too kind and selfless to go through this life alone." She shocks me by hugging me tight. "Value her for who she is and not *who* she is."

I return her hug and release her. "Can I ask you a question?"

She gives me a weary look. "Okay?"

"Why doesn't Nate like her?" I test her knowledge on her fiancé's dislike.

Mariah grimaces. "It's that noticeable?"

"Yea, and sure I'm not the only one who has." I give her a meaningful look. As if she can hear us talking about her Elsie turns and gives both of us a bright smile.

"He is having a hard time sharing my attention. It is a new development and I'm not sure how to mend the rift." She looks up at me, sadness etched in her features.

I squeeze her arm. "It's okay. We will figure it out," I reassure her with a united front. At least she knows what the root of the issue is. That is half the battle.

"Figure what out?" Elsie's voice is light and full of excitement.

"When a good time to meet my sister would be." I gesture to Natalie standing a few feet away checking out the books on the shelf.

Elsie's gaze follows my gesture, her smile could light up even the darkest cavern. She takes a moment to walk over to stand next to my sister. Who is totally enthralled with the travel book on Germany. Elsie picks up an identical book. "What city would you recommend I visit first?"

Natalie keeps her eyes on her book. "I haven't been myself."

"Maybe I could take another assistant the next time I go for an event." Elsie closes the book in her hand and places it back on the shelf.

Natalie slams her book shut as she looks at Elsie. "Oh my God!" She barely refrains from screaming. "Oh my God! You're talking to me. It's you, you're talking to me." Natalie's eyes are as round as they can go.

Elsie laughs. "It's me. Of course, I'm talking to you. Would you like to be my assistant on one of my signings abroad?"

"You can't ask me that! You don't know me!" Tears brim her eyes as she looks at her favorite author.

"Well, that is true. But you see, someone I know well, he vouches for you. I trust his judgement. So, if he trusts you, I trust you. Plus, you have excellent taste in books." She laughs.

"Can I hug you?" Natalie is practically vibrating with excitement.

"Of course, you can!" Natalie lets out a squeal of delight as she pulls Elsie into a hard hug.

"Aw, look your soon to be sister-in-law approves of you!" Mariah teases as she moves past us to address the crowed.

Natalie stills, and slowly pulls back from Elsie. Apprehension paramount on her face. "Sister-in-law?" She looks at me closely. "I thought you were just interested in getting to know her."

Elsie disengages completely. She looks up at me, with a shy smile before offering Natalie a quick hug as she moves to head to the tables. . "I'll leave you both to it, please feel free to sit back here for the Q and A. After it is over if you have a question you would like to ask I will answer anything."

I watch Elsie walk over to the table where Mariah is speaking to the crowd. "If those of you with a question would form a line to the left we would appreciate it." Several people in the gathering move to the side to wait for their question to be answered. "We can't guarantee all of you will get to ask your questions, but we will get through as many as time allows."

Natalie moves to stand in front of me. "What happened to just getting to know her?" Her tone is guarded. "What did you do, make sure she was who you thought she was and just proposed right there? How on earth did she agree to anything like that?" Natalie's eyes brim with tears as her emotions grab hold.

I hug my sister to me. "I was watching her, and she got harassed. I stepped in and said she was my fiancé. She played along. The man must have called and told someone who told someone. Her PR called her and mine called me, and they both agree we should play this up for a while. Elsie is game." I shrug as I release my sister.

She looks up at me. "But...?"

I sigh, "I am going to do everything I can to get Elsie to fall in love with me. She is just as easy in person as she is online to talk to. I like who she is." Natalie grins and takes my hand as we move towards our seats.

"She might be harder to win than you think." Natalie whispers. "Or what if you find out something about her that you just can't handle?"

"I'm not a twenty-year-old frat boy. I like to think I have enough sense to realize there is something extraordinary about Elsie. My world feels more right with her physically in it."

Natalie squeezes my hand as the crowd quiets down.

Mariah moves to take a seat while Elsie stands and picks up a microphone. "Good evening everyone. I am so grateful that you decided to share your time with me tonight!" She walks down the length of the tables they have set out for her. "Let's jump right into it then! What is your question tonight?"

A young teen steps forward, her hair is cut short and tucked behind her ears. Her glasses make her look younger and vulnerable. I shift in my seat next to my sister and wait for the woman to speak.

"Hi, my question tonight is, I want to be a writer. Where do I start?" Her voice is soft, the microphone barely amplifies it to a normal speaking voice. She pushes her glasses back up her nose as she fidgets from one foot to the other, waiting for Elsie.

"Have you written anything of the story in your heart?" Elsie's tone is friendly.

"I have. I am about four chapters in," the girl answers.

"What is your name?" Elsie tilts her head as she asks.

"My name is Autumn. Autumn Foley."

"Would you please come here?" The girl takes a step back, a moment of sheer panic crosses her face. Elsie smiles and holds out her hand to the teen. With a determined nod the teen takes the fifteen or so steps to Elsie's table. Elsie hands her an index card and a permanent marker. She puts down the microphone, switching it off as she does. Natalie and I share a glance before we lean closer to hear the exchange.

"May I have your autograph?" Elsie holds out the paper and marker. The teen looks at Elsie with utter confusion. "I am so pleased to meet a fellow writer. Write what makes your heart happy. You don't need a contract and money to prove yourself. You are someone. You are enough, just the way you are."

The teen smiles as tears fall down her face. She takes the card and signs it. Elsie takes it and hands her another card. "When you finish your story please send it to me. I would love to read it and help you more if *you* want." Her emphasis on you is direct. The teen nods.

"Thank you so much, you will never understand how finding

you and your writing has changed my life." She leans across the table to hug Elsie. She moves quickly to reclaim her seat in the audience.

Elsie makes a quick note on the back of the card and places it on the table in front of her. She grabs the mic and turns it back on, "All y'all remember her, she's going to do amazing things one day." She winks at the teen. "Who has another question?"

A gray-haired woman steps up. "When you started writing at such a young age did you dream of having your own family one day, like the couples in your stories?" The older woman smiles wide.

"I have a family. All of you support my dreams. I have a sister in Mariah." She turns to smile at Mariah. Her gaze flits to mine and her blush creeps up her face. She turns back to the woman. "We might not be related but we are loyal, honest, and love each other unconditionally. I have achieved all the dreams I have ever allowed myself to have."

Mariah's tears are silent. "And I have Nate. Mariah's other half, who very soon will become like my brother-in-law. I couldn't be happier for them." Elsie smiles lovingly at Mariah. "This is all the family I have ever hoped to have, then and now, and I feel so honored to have them." The woman and dabs her own eyes. She finds her seat.

"You have said this is your last book in Kismet Summers, what will your next series be, have you thought of writing another genre?"

Elsie fans herself. "Well that is a couple of questions." She laughs. "Okay, let's see. This is my last book in this series. I have thought about writing paranormal but my outlines of late tend to be more in the fantasy line than paranormal. I'm not for sure yet. I have a few projects in the works for screen plays so we will see what comes of those."

"What is your idea of a perfect date?" the next woman asks. She is about Elsie's age with brown hair and a dark dress.

"Why? Wanna ask me out?" Elsie teases, the congregation

laughs. "Perfect date? To be totally honest I was just asked on my first date today. Up until recently I had not put myself out there because if I got my heart obliterated it might change my light approach to romance and then where would any of us be?"

"So, you are officially seeing someone?" the questioner speaks again.

"Actually, I'm sure most of you have already heard, I recently got engaged." Elsie keeps her face to the crowd, but I see her glace sideways toward me. The crowd murmurs, a loud applause comes from all of them. "Would you all like to meet him?" She raises an eyebrow, before turning to me. "Darling, would you come say hello to these wonderful people?"

I can't help the smile as I stand and make my way to her side. "What do you think? Is he handsome enough?"

Everyone stands and claps. Elsie turns to me, her expression pure happiness. I reach for her. With minimal effort I tip her back and kiss her. She is mid laugh as my lips meet hers. I make sure to keep it PG. I steady her as I stand her back upright, my hand stays on her waist.

"You're not mad I brought you out in the open with my fans?" she whispers.

"I am finding that I like being next to you." I kiss her cheek and squeeze her side.

CHAPTER 24

*E*LSIE

My stomach unclenches. The anxiety ball I was nursing inside dissipates. Bradley's voice has always had the ability to calm my anxiety whenever we talked online, in person he is lethal to that pesky trait of mine. Normally, I don't like being hugged or touched, but it feels like my world is right with Bradley. I find that revelation both alarming and exhilarating.

"Okay, who has the next question?" I bring the event back to order and turn to look up at Bradley. "You can sit if you'd like."

"How about I go get you a muffin to pick at, you can't live off coffee alone." He kisses my cheek again before he turns to make his way to the café.

"Top favorite romantic movies!" Another teen is clutching a graphic novel of mine.

"Oh, I'll give you my top five love stories. One: *You've Got Mail*. Two: *Letters to Juliette*. Three: *Jane Austen Book Club*. Four: *Gone with the Wind*. Five: *The Godfather*. And before you all get on my case about *The Godfather* let me defend myself. *The Godfather* is the ultimate family story. You don't need to be born into their family. You just have to be loyal." I sigh. "So, much love for their parents and their children." That answer must be enough because the young woman nods and returns to her seat.

"Hi! I'm Rebekkah. I am dying to know what's the most influential book you have read."

"Glad to meet you, Rebekkah." I think for a moment. "Okay, so my very first book that ever got me thinking about being a writer was *Ella Enchanted*. I still have the first five chapters of that book memorized. As I have gotten older Jane Austen became my personal hero. She wrote amazing love stories that have transcended time and yet she never knew love or was married."

The next person is a woman with bright pink hair. "Hi! I'm Ashley, or as you know me, Mizbehavin. I have a new question for you."

My heart sinks a little. I thought her original question was interesting. "Welcome! I'm glad to finally meet you!"

"So, you once said in an interview that you play videogames. Since I know first-hand that you play *Annex*, I am curious if you play any other games, or have you read the *Annex* books?"

"Yes. I do play online games. I love puzzle games. I play *The Room* series. I also hate to admit that I play a phone app game to keep my vocabulary skills sharp. But the one I spend over twenty hours a week on is *Annex*. I fully blame my insomnia on *Annex*. I have played it since the beta. Of course, I have read the series. It is amazing. I recommend it to anyone who loves to read fantasy."

Mariah taps me on the shoulder. "We have time for one more question and then we need to move on to the signing."

"Okay, one more question tonight." I smile at the small girl up next. "Do you read my books?"

She nods. "My mother says you are appropriate to read because you are not vulgar."

I smile at her. "Which is your favorite one?"

The girl is silent for a moment. "I love Mariah and Nate's story in, *Finding My Forever*."

I nod. "That is one of my favorites too." I look at Mariah who smiles at me. "What is your question?"

She clears her throat, "Do you have a favorite snack you eat while you write, or special music you play?"

"That is a great question!" Bradley places a muffin in front of me, I look up at him and mouth 'thank you'. I look back at the girl to answer her, "I drink a lot of death wish coffee. I always have peanut butter M&Ms on my desk. Once in a blue moon I will switch my coffee for a cold Coca Cola. I tend to write all night and I play music based on the tone of my story as opposed to my mood. If music doesn't work, then I toss on one of my favorite movies and write."

With that Mariah stands, I hand my mic to her as I sit. I make sure my space is organized as she gets the assembly in order. "If everyone would please form a single file line, it will help the process. A few of us will be coming around to write your name on a Post-It note in case you want anything personalized. We appreciate you all coming out."

I take a quick bite of the muffin and suck down half of the iced coffee in front of me. I take note of the time, it is eight thirty. Mariah comes over. "Hey, you ready for this?" I stand back up to be level with her.

I smile at her. "If I say no will you whisk me away?"

"No, but I will feign injury and demand an evacuation." She kisses my cheek.

"Could you make sure Derrik knows he doesn't have to stick around. I don't think he knows how long this could take." I am proud of myself for remembering to call him Derrik. It is sobering to see how tedious remembering the change his name is. I feel sorry for Mariah that I have made her do it for so long.

Mariah looks over at the man, "I will tell him, but I doubt he will listen. I think he is really into you." She looks back at me to catch me rolling my eyes at her. "I brought you an overnight bag and your laptop so you can crash at a hotel with us." I glance to where she is pointing. I see my Raven, House of Flynn bag under the table I will be sitting at.

"I love you most. What would I do without you?"

"Probably sleep on the floor of the bookstore after your event." She laughs and moves to go make post-its for me, stopping only to relay the message to Bradley. His expression is grim as he looks out over the large group. I take my seat once more. Before I gesture for the first fan to come up for me to sign, I pop the last bite of my muffin into my mouth and wash it down with the last of my coffee.

CHAPTER 25

*B*RADLEY

I watch Elsie inhale the last bite of the muffin and the rest of her iced coffee before she takes the first fan's book to sign. I scan the crowd; there must be well over two hundred people here. I watch her sign three people and the next woman up hands Elsie book after book to sign.

"She will literally sign anything you want her to." Natalie says, her gaze following mine to the woman now on item eight for Elsie to sign.

"How long do these normally last?"

"The last one I went to I was about the middle of the line to get something signed. It was about eleven-thirty when I got through the line to her." Natalie looks at me. "I was the middle of the line." She repeats.

"When did that event start?"

"About the same as this one. She started signing around eight." Natalie glances at the clock opposite the wall. "Do you want my advice?"

I scrub my hand over my face. "Is it about Elsie?"

She nods.

"Always." I look at Elsie before looking back at my sister. "I will always want your advice when it comes to her."

Natalie smiles a little. "Stay. Get her another iced coffee, get her another muffin. Offer her some Tylenol."

I give her a quizzical look. "Tylenol?"

Natalie looks at me like I have three heads all of a sudden, "Are you that thick?" She shakes her head, "Her hand is going to start to hurt soon."

I feel stupid. "Right."

"Also, you might want to ask her assistant if Elsie has accommodations for tonight." My sister tilts her head as she looks over at Elsie. "She has a bag under the table so she must be anticipating grabbing a hotel room after this event."

"A hotel room?" Natalie laughs at the tone in my voice.

"Bradley, she probably won't be done with this event until after one in the morning."

I pull out my phone and call the Hyatt. "Yes, this is Derrik Derrikson. I need a room for tonight and tomorrow night." Natalie moves her hand to get my attention, but the woman taking my reservation speaks first.

"Sir, we have no vacancy." Her voice is soft, I hear her typing on a keyboard. "Unless you are interested in the penthouse."

"Perfect. Please have a set of robes sent up. I will be checking in within the next couple of hours." I hang up after I get my confirmation. I look at my sister. "What?"

"Elsie is not one of your trashy girlfriends."

"No, she is perfect." I offer my sister a smile.

"Then don't treat her like one of your usual girls." She looks at me with a hard stare. "I mean it. Don't try to get her into bed or anything. It will not end well for you. She will run and you will lose her forever."

I glance at Elsie. I watch her carefully flex her hand. I take that as my queue. "Got any Tylenol?" I ask my sister. She places a bottle in my hand without a word. I make the coffee café my first stop where there is no one in line.

"Sir, we are closing in fifteen minutes."

"Perfect can you make me two large iced mochas with two shots of espresso in them? And can I get another blueberry muffin?"

"We are out of blueberry, but we do have a chocolate left."

I nod. I turn to watch Elsie while I wait. "I'm glad someone is watching out for her. Last time she came the crowd was only about a third of what it is today and the poor girl about passed out by the end of it." The young girl behind the counter handed me my items. "I'm glad she has someone to look out for her this year."

"She does this yearly?" I ask as I grab napkins.

"She has for the last five years." The girl turns to start shutting down the machines.

It only takes me a couple of seconds to make my way to Elsie's side. I place the fresh coffee in front of her and a new muffin. "Here, take these." I offer her two Tylenol.

She looks up at me; her eyes aren't as bright as they had been earlier. She looks anxious. Her gaze flits to my hand and the pills. Elsie puts her pen down, shakes her hand vigorously, and takes the offered pills. She takes a long drink of her coffee.

Taking the opportunity to sit down in the chair next to her I whisper, "Are you okay?"

She studies me for a moment. "I need you to go in my bag at my feet and get my Xanax out for me. I'm having a panic attack and I am not sure how much longer I can keep it together." Her whisper is fast and forced.

I drop to the floor next to her legs and pull her bag to me. Without hesitation I unzip it, I move the things inside around. Something soft and cold slides easily around my hand. There is a lot of silk in this bag. I push the thought out of my mind and keep blindly searching for a pill bottle. I feel one and pull it out. I put it in her lap in case she is self-conscious over needing it. "Is this the right medication?" She gives me one quick nod. I grab the bottle and pull one pill out. I reach out for her hand and place the pill in it. She checks her hand before she takes it quickly without skipping a beat of the signing. It takes minimal effort to pull myself back up into the empty chair next to her.

Elsie stands to stretch. Mariah comes over quickly to pull Elsie close to her. It almost looks like a hug, but it is different. The closer I watch the more obvious it isn't just a hug. Mariah has a firm hold on Elsie, she is breathing deliberately, in a very pronounced way. Elsie is taking two breaths to Mariah's one. I hear Mariah murmuring to Elsie, but the words are too low for me to decipher. The hug only lasts a couple of minutes. None of the fans in line seem to mind waiting for their author. Finally, Elsie is breathing in sync with Mariah. Gradually Mariah softens her hold. The whole scene makes me envious that I'm not the one comforting Elsie. Part of me also realizes that I wouldn't have known to do any of that if we had been alone. I make a note of how to handle her panic in the future. Maybe Mariah can tell me what kind of triggers she has.

"Crowds and people hugging her." My sister answers my unspoken thoughts.

"How did you know that is what I was thinking?" I whisper without taking my eyes off Mariah and Elsie.

"Because you are concentrating so hard, I think the hamster in your head might die from being overworked." She softly laughs.

"I had no idea she had a panic disorder," I admit. She's never mentioned it online and never had one during any chats.

"Does it make you like her less?" Her question catches me off guard. I tear my gaze away from the women.

"Why would it?" I run my hand over my hair, "I was just trying to make a note of how Mariah is calming her down so I might know what to do if it ever happens in the future."

My sister gives me the biggest smile I have ever seen on her. "You really like her, don't you?"

I turn my attention back to Elsie. She disengages from Mariah and the fans in line all clap hard for her as she sits back down to resume the signing. Natalie and I sit in silence as the event carries on. My gaze is locked on Elsie watching for any signs of distress or discomfort. I hear my sister yawn next to me, instinctually I check my watch, it is after midnight already. The line thankfully is over the halfway mark.

We sit and watch as the line slowly gets shorter and shorter. An idea sparks in my brain, which evolves into a full-fledged plan. I pull my phone out to call the hotel again. "Yes, Hello. I just called about a room. I am actually going to need it until Friday." Once again, I am left waiting for the receptionist to give me confirmation that I can have the room. When the answer I want is given I hang up and look at my sister.

"What are you planning over there?" she asks as I put my phone back in my pocket.

"I think Elsie needs to relax and not be rushed back to wherever they are having her stay. Besides, it would be a shame not to show off my company to a loyal fan." I smile at her.

Natalie rolls her dark eyes. "It also doesn't hurt you are into her and that she is amazingly beautiful..." Her tone trails off waiting for me to contradict her. It never comes.

"All facts." My attention is again pulled to the signing area as Mariah picks of the microphone.

"We want to thank each and every one of you for coming out and spending your night with our beloved Elsie." There are about fifty people left in line for Elsie. Mariah switches off the microphone, she turns to head towards me and my sister. Before she can make it three steps towards us she is intercepted by the looming presence of Mr. Antik. The man is already on my nerves.

"We need to finish closing our registers down; will Ms. Williams be ready to check her items out soon?" His tone is quiet, but he does not sound pleasant.

I move to stand between him and yet another woman for the second time today. "I'll take care of her items now; that's no problem."

Mr. Antik gives me a quick once over before leading the way to the register to check out the items she has on hold. Her books take four bags. "That will be $632.07, sir." I hand the man my card as I turn to check on the woman who has become as important to me as breathing in this short amount of time. "Here you go." I turn back to him to retrieve my card. I take the bags without another word to the man who has tossed our lives into turmoil. Maybe I should thank him for his aggressive approach earlier. It did get me closer to Elsie. But then I remember her saying how being approached like that made her feel and I feel mad all over again.

"You okay?" Natalie gives me a critical appraisal.

"Just annoyed with that manager. He is too aggressive." I huff. Setting the bags on the floor next to the chairs we had been sitting in the whole event. I notice the last fan is getting their books signed and as they walk away Elsie finally puts her pen down. She leans forward and puts her head on the table, her nondominant hand cradles her other. Before I can react, Mariah beats me to her.

"Hey, you okay?" She kneels next to Elsie's chair. Her hand pats her best friend on the back softly. "You can come with Nate and me. We can share a bed again." She grabs the handle of the overnight bag as she stands up.

Here is my queue. I walk to them with my hand out for the bag. "I got her. You go relax with your man." Mariah looks from me to Elsie, distress etched in her eyes.

Elsie takes her time to lift her head off the table. Very carefully she stands up, her gaze looks from Mariah and lifts to mine, "You have room for me?"

"I booked a hotel hours ago."

Elsie frowns. "I won't sleep with you."

"No. I expect you to relax and sleep for as long as you need to." I give her my best smile. Natalie's expression is smug, as if she knew Elsie would say something like that. "Booked it for the rest of the week."

CHAPTER 26

E<u>LSIE</u>

His smile makes me lose sense of time and circumstances for a moment. I shrug as I look back at Mariah. "I guess I have somewhere to stay tonight."

"You sure you're okay staying with someone you just met?" Mariah looks at Bradley then back to me.

I smile at my closest friend before I lean forward and kiss Mariah on the cheek. "I've known Derrik for two years. We have spent over two thousand hours together."

"I have a room at the Hyatt. I promise to be on my best behavior." Bradley holds up his hand in a scout honor salute.

"If you need me, call me. I don't care what time it is. Do you hear me?" Mariah grabs my hands in hers.

"I know." I try my best to reassure her.

"I love you water sister." She says as Nate comes over to take her hand. She opens her other hand. "Pick one." It is the fortune cookies from our dinner.

"Like blood." I pick one of the little packages. Bradley snatches one too. I blow her a kiss as Nate turns them to walk to the exit.

"Ready?" Bradley asks as he watches the couple exit.

Finally, I turn to him. He has four shopping bags, the bags from the dress store, and my House of Flynn bag in his hands. I move to take my overnight bag from him, but he moves the bag away from my grasp. "I can carry something."

"I got it. Come on, let's get out of here." He smiles at me again.

All I have energy to do is nod as I turn to make my way to the exit. Bradley puts my overnight bag on his shoulder and holds the bags in one hand. His free hand rests on my hip as we walk out of the bookstore.

"Natalie, do you need a ride or are you good?" He turns his head to find his sister.

"I could use a ride if it isn't too much trouble." Her voice is thick, she is struggling to keep her eyes open. "Guess I should move your schedule around the rest of the week." She smiles at her brother.

"You don't need to do anything special. I will travel back to the house I rented tomorrow," I interject.

"Do you have anything going on in the next three days?" Bradley's voice is soft as he leads us to his black charger. He unlocks the doors as he goes to the trunk to toss all of my bags in.

"I owe you for all my crazy shopping today." I take the passenger seat since Natalie takes the backseat before I get a chance to. As I pull on the door to close it, Bradley pulls the door back and out of the grasp.

He leans down, his gaze level with mine. "I need you to stop worrying about things. I don't do anything I don't want to." His fingers thread into my hair as he pulls me to his mouth. His kiss sears and comforts. I lose myself to it. I hear someone clear their throat and my brain reminds me that we are not alone. Bradley holds me as he deepens the kiss. My nails comb through his hair. Slowly, he brings me down and breaks the contact. His nose still next to mine, his eyes still closed. "Just relax. Trust me." He opens his eyes. "Can you do that?"

I tilt my head. I can't help the smile that comes. "I will try my best." I peck him lightly on the lips before I pull away, averting my gaze. Out of the corner of my eye I see Bradley stand. He closes the car door. Within a few seconds he is in the driver seat. I hear the click of his seatbelt, then the roar of the engine starting. I lean my head back on the seat, my eyes are too heavy to keep open. I hear the low voices of Bradley and Natalie but I'm too tired to listen.

CHAPTER 27

$\mathcal{B}$RADLEY

"I've never seen you so enthralled with anyone in my life." Natalie's voice is quiet as her gaze locks on mine in the rearview mirror.

I look over at Elsie. She looks so peaceful. It humbles me that she can be so relaxed that she can fall asleep in a car with someone she just met in person.

"Are you scared?" Natalie's question has my attention diverted back to her.

I concentrate on the road. Am I scared? I search my mind and heart. "I'm scared I am going to mess this up. That I will lose her after I finally found her."

"Found her?"

I glance at Elsie again before turning my focus back to the road. I nod. "I feel like my life is complete. My world is perfect now that she is in it."

Natalie looks out her window and wipes her face with her fingers.

"You okay?" I look at her in the mirror before putting on my turn signal to pull over in front of her condo.

"You're my favorite brother. I am just so happy you have

found someone I one hundred percent like for you." She opens her door, with her body turned sideways to get out, "I am rooting for you both." With that she stands, closes the door, and walks up to her door. She waves as she opens the door. I honk as I prepare to drive away. I watch her enter and close her door before I head toward the hotel. The drive is silent as I let Elsie sleep. It's silent and I'm alone with my thoughts. Maybe I counted my chickens too quickly on the silent part, and the alone with my thoughts part.

"Where are we going?" Elsie's voice is soft and full of sleep. I'm not convinced she is awake. I steal a glance at her to verify she isn't talking in her sleep. Her eyes open slowly to look at me.

"I booked a spot in the Hyatt. I'd take you back to my place, but I'm in no condition to make the seventy-minute drive." My answer seems to be enough. Elsie's eyes close once more. "Would you like me to stop somewhere and pick up some food? I think a few places close by are open still."

"I'm not hungry. I'll be fine. I just need to rest my eyes for a couple of minutes." Her eyes remain closed even as she answers me. We are only a few blocks from the hotel when Elsie's phone rings. I hear her sigh as she moves to grab and answer it. "No," she answers, she sounds exhausted. After a few seconds she groans. "Do I have to do that right now?" She sits up, phone still in her hand. Elsie pushes the speaker button as she starts looking around.

"Yes, it is bad luck if you don't!" Mariah's voice is slightly louder than usual. "C'mon, I already opened mine!" She whines.

There is a crinkling of plastic as Elsie finds her fortune cookie from dinner. I pull into the lot of the hotel and park. "Okay, what does yours say?" Elsie looks at me before she rolls her eyes, and mouths sorry to me as she waits. I offer a smile. I'm not in a rush.

"Mine says, 'a new voyage will fill your life with untold memories'." Mariah sighs a little. "Isn't that stupid spot on?" She waits. "Now what does yours say?"

"I just don't see why this is always so important to you." Elsie shakes her head as she opens her cookie.

"Remember when you first came to live with us?" Mariah urges.

"Yea."

"That first night we had Chinese for dinner, because my parents asked you what you wanted to eat." She pauses. "And our fortunes that night matched. They said, 'Family is not always...'"

"Who you think it is." Elsie whispers. "Yes, I remember."

"So, what does yours say?" Mariah prods.

Elsie takes the little paper out; it takes her a second to read. She laughs, but the sound dies as she glances at me. Her eyes widen. "Um, mine says 'all your hard work will soon pay off'."

"Bullshit! That is what yours said last time." Mariah pushes back. "What does it really say?"

Elsie licks her lip. "It says, 'stop searching for forever. Happiness is just next to you.'"

Mariah quietly squeals. "He's sitting next to you, isn't he?"

"I have to go." She hangs up before saying anything else. She powers off her phone before she looks at me again. "I need some Tylenol."

"Don't you want to know what mine says?" I keep my voice low.

CHAPTER 28

$\mathcal{E}$LSIE

"I hope it is something really mundane." I can't help but smile at him.

His eyes search my face. He doesn't move, except to turn off the car. "You sure you don't want me to go grab some food?"

I shake my head. "What does your fortune say?"

He looks away from me, I hear the familiar crinkle as he pulls his cookie out of his pocket. He glances at me before he pulls the slip of paper out to read. "Follow the advice of your heart." His voice is low, I can almost feel the vibration of his baritone in the air.

I take this opportunity to open the car door so I can get out before we do something we will both regret. He meets me at the trunk where my bags are. "I got these."

"Let me at least carry my overnight bag, so I don't feel like I'm useless." I flash him a pout like I have seen Mariah do to get Nate to agree to something.

As I reach for my bag Bradley pulls me to him, his mouth catches mine, it is soft but firm. He possesses me. I can't help the moan that escapes as I comb my fingers in his hair. I am too enthralled to think beyond this kiss. His fingers play with my hair, his tongue is a welcome invasion.

I hear clicking, which pulls me out of the moment. Bradley and I disengage slowly to find four or five photographers close with their cameras snapping away. He makes quick work of grabbing the bags and pulling me into the hotel leaving the vultures outside the main doors. My heart sinks. I'm the center of attention, right where I don't want to ever be.

"Good evening, sir." A tall, slender blonde greets Bradley. "How may I help you?" She flashes a perfect smile.

"My fiancé and I need to check in," Bradley answers. "Here is the card I want to have on file for any charges for our room."

"Yes, sir." Her gaze sweeps up and down me, a small smile appears on her lips before she returns to her computer. "Is there anything else I can do for you?"

"No, I think we have everything we need for tonight." She slides a little paper sleeve with our key cards in them.

"Hope you enjoy your stay with us," she calls as Bradley turns us toward the elevators. I follow him without paying too much attention to the hotel or where we are going.

"She was pretty," I comment as the elevator doors close to take us to our room.

"Was she?" He tilts his head to look at me.

I roll my eyes. "Sorry to disappoint you, but it would take more than someone mildly flirting with you to get me even a little jealous."

His gaze bores into mine. "I have never in my life cheated on anyone I have ever been in a relationship with."

I can't help but smile. "I have no way of knowing if that is the truth." I shrug. "I am going off blind faith."

"Doesn't everyone who is newly dating?" His question hangs in the air. The elevator dings, and the doors open. There is a long, polished floor leading to one lone door on the floor. Bradley steps into the hall with me, he puts the bags down outside the door. I hear the click of the lock disengaging then I am lifted. Laughter escapes as Bradley picks me up to carry me into the room like a blushing bride. I shake my head to dispel the imagery. He puts me down inside the room. It seems to go on forever.

"I've never seen a hotel room like this before." I am afraid to speak loud in such a grand place.

I turn around to see Bradley closing the door, bags in his hands. "Do you approve?" He looks a little uncertain as he looks around. He finds a panel of switches for the lights. My attention is pulled in every direction as I get my bearings. The room we came into from the door is apparently a living room. There are two long couches, a tv stand, and coffee table. The far wall is lined with floor to ceiling windows. The view is incredible. "I like it very much, indeed." I answer as I turn back to look at him. Relief washes over his features.

"Here, let's get you all figured out. I'm sure you are exhausted." He holds out his hand for me to take. Without hesitation I grab my overnight bag with one hand and take his with my other. Hand in hand we walk down a small hallway to find two bedrooms. They both share a large bathroom. My nagging trepidation is assuaged for a moment seeing two bedrooms.

"Thank you." I open a door to a large king size bed. "Um, would you rather have this room?"

He looks at me, his perfect brow furrows. "Why? Don't you like it?"

$\mathcal{B}$RADLEY

She worries her bottom lip as she avoids my gaze. "The bed is bigger than I am used to." She looks up at me, "I'm not sure if I will sleep with so much space around me." Elsie moves to open the other bedroom door. I already know from booking the room that it is a smaller bed. "Do you mind if I take this one?"

I shrug. "Whatever you prefer. Makes no difference to me."

She nods. As she walks into her room. I leave her to herself. I have never been so glad to have great forethought in my whole life. My own overnight bag is next to her shopping bags from earlier. As I make my way to my room I can feel how exhausted I am, but a bigger part of me doesn't want to miss a moment with Elsie. I don't bother unpacking my bag, I toss it into a chair in the corner of my room. The door that leads to the shared bathroom is open, light on, Elsie in front of the mirror. I can only see her profile since the sink is the only visible thing in the room when the door is open. She is brushing her teeth. She leans forward and takes a sip from the running water in the sink. I decide to retrieve my own toothbrush from my bag. I turn around to find Elsie in the bathroom doorway into my room.

"Do you mind if I take a shower?" A soft blush settles on her cheeks.

"Please." I gesture to the bathroom. "Mind if I brush my teeth while you do?"

She glances to the other side of the bathroom. "Sure as soon as you hear the water running you can come in then. Does that work for you?" She looks a little worried.

"I can wait if it bothers you," I offer.

She shakes her head. "No, it's fine. I'm used to sharing a bathroom."

"With a man?" I raise a skeptical brow.

"Well, yes." All humor is gone from her face. "I normally have to crash with Mariah and Nate when I have a signing."

My brow furrows. "Nate comes in the bathroom while you are showering?"

"Sometimes. Most of the time the only room available has just one bed for all three of us. So we can brush our teeth or go to the bathroom while someone showers. That way we get done and can sleep sooner." She gives me a hard stare. "I know he isn't into me. If anything I annoy him."

"How are you so sure?"

Her own brow furrows as she looks away for a moment. As if thinking of how she knows or trying to find the words. "Nate and Mariah have been together since forever. Even if he did have any interest the feelings have never been returned. He is like a brother to me." She takes a deep breath. "Besides, when there is only one bed I typically take a shower and either write or read."

"You sit and write or read while they sleep? I can't help but smile at the odd picture that puts into my head.

She giggles. "No, I literally go down to the lobby of the hotel and write or read.."

"Why?"

"I wasn't kidding when I say I have insomnia." With that she turns to go into her room. In seconds she walks into the bathroom with clothes and some bottles. Maybe I should find something to sleep in. Normally, I pack my overnight to crash in my sister's condo or at the office if we have an extensive patch to perform on *Annex*. As I search for suitable sleepwear, I hear music come on. I close my eyes preparing my senses to be assaulted. I have no idea what kind of music she listens to when she is alone. What if it is horrible? What if it is a deal breaker? I quickly think of the worst music I can think of to gauge if I have a limit on music taste. Before I can think of the worst, I hear some country ballad about breaking up. I relax a little. I can handle some country. As I hear the water start signaling it is safe to go in, I remember an earlier question she was asked. About music she listens to. Her answer was "I play music based on the tone of my story as opposed to my mood." Does that hold true for when she isn't writing?

I shake my head and go to brush my teeth. My heart almost stops, the shower has frosted glass doors. Elsie is washing her hair, head tilted back, hands in her hair. The typical sexy pose but it looks so much sexier from her. The song ends as I finish with my teeth. The next one is a pop song about falling in love out of the blue. I look down at the counter and see there is a little glass toothbrush holder with Elsie's in it. I place mine next to it. I realize I am a mess when it comes to this woman. I'm about to leave the room when I hear her voice.

"Um... Bradley?" Her voice falters a little.

"Yes?"

"Could you please hand me a towel?"

I chuckle and thank the stars for aligning. She slides the glass door a few inches, her hand comes out. I hand her a big fluffy white towel. "Thank you." Her voice is soft.

"Anytime," I answer as I make my way back to the door to my room. Before I make it, the shower door slides open to reveal the vision that is Elsie. Her dark hair is slick, the towel looks like a runway dress on her. "I was just leaving." I try to make my voice sound normal.

She nods as she watches me leave. I close the door behind me to give her privacy. The song finally changes to an odd song that I hear Elsie singing along to. It is catchy but not something I am familiar with. It seems to be longer than normal songs. Another upbeat song she starts singing to while the hairdryer turns on starts next. Finally, the machine is turned off as I hear her voice in the hallway singing along to a remake of some song about having an affair. I follow her.

As I come out of my room, I see Elsie bend to grab the bags from her shopping earlier. She stands and the breath in my lungs turns to ash. I knew I felt silk in that bag earlier when I was looking for her Xanax. She has a long, black silk nightgown on. The bottom of the gown almost touches the floor. She sees me looking, the blush creeps up her cheeks.

"Sorry, this is what I typically sleep in when I'm alone." She keeps her eyes on the floor, accepting the judgement coming.

I walk to her with purpose. As gently as I can I use my finger to tilt her face up to look at me. Her eyes search mine for a moment, hesitantly I close the space between our lips. Elsie wraps her arms around my neck as I put my own around her. Gently I pull her closer to me. The softness of her nightgown is nothing to the feel of her body flush against mine. I reach up to tangle my fingers of one of my hands in her hair. Elsie keeps up with my pace, I tug her hair to pull her head back a little. Her neck is too enticing to leave untouched. Slowly I trail kisses from her lips, down her neck to her shoulder. She moves on her own to give me access.

"Hmmm." She breathes. "Bradley, I need to get back to my room." Her body betrays her. Her fingers play with my hair, carefully keeping my lips on her skin.

"Do you want me to stop?" I retrace the path my lips made with my tongue.

"I can't do this," she whispers.

Instantly I stop. I only hold her to make sure she has her footing. When I am sure she can stand without assistance I drop my hands from her.

"Can we talk about this?" she whispers.

Taken slightly aback, I nod. Having a woman turn me down is new, but so is having a woman who wants to talk instead of making me play the 'what pissed me off today' game.

I follow her into the living room. Elsie sits in the corner of the couch her legs curled under her. She rests her chin on her hand as she watches me. I take a seat on the couch opposite her. She takes a deep breath, "I've never had a relationship before," she admits. She has said that before but hearing it while we are alone makes me actually hear her this time.

"Like you've never..." I let me voice trail off, but I keep my eyes on her.

"Does that matter?" I can't tell by her tone if she is worried or vexed.

"No." The answer is immediate but as I think about the possibility, I can't help feeling more turned on thinking I might be her first. If she would let me.

"What kind of romance author would I be if I haven't at least had sex?" She gifts me a small smile. She sits up a little taller. "I've had sex. Once. I know the importance of the stories I write. It is for women, like me, who dream of it being better than it is."

"You only did it once?"

"I needed to feel wanted, just for a little bit." Her voice is a whisper. "But, you know what they say, 'be careful what you wish for.'" She purses her lips. She sighs. "And that is why I write." Her hand plays with her hair. "I have never felt anything like what I feel when you are near. It's scary and exhilarating." She releases her hair to look at me, "I'm not ready to lose that."

"Why would you have to lose anything?" I keep my tone light.

"Because if I give you what you want then you have no reason to stay."

Before she can get off the couch or say another word I move to kneel in front of her. Her face feels natural in my hands as I cup her face. "If you told me you were saving yourself for marriage I would book two first class tickets to Vegas right now."

Her eyes widen. "You don't know me."

"I know enough that I am certain we would be amazing together, both physically and mentally."

She tries to shake her head. "But sooner or later you would tire of me, or we would disagree on something substantial, and you'd call it quits." Tears spring to her eyes. "I don't believe in divorce. I don't want to be just a notch in someone's bedpost."

My thumbs wipe the tears off her face as my lips meet hers in a soft kiss. I pull back to look at her. Her eyes open, "What if we just treat this like the two-year relationship that it is and let it go wherever feels right?" My voice is a whisper. I hold my breath waiting for her to decide.

CHAPTER 30

$\mathcal{E}$LSIE

Can I really marry the thought that Bradley is Thorantik? That the two years we have been talking online could equate to time in real life?

He waits for me to answer him. I know how romance goes in my books. The formula is absolute. Real life is a horse of a different color. I move out of his touch to clear my own head.

"What is the longest relationship you have ever had?" I feel like I need to know more information to make the right decision for me.

He studies me. "Aside from you?"

I roll my eyes. "Yes, what is the longest girlfriend you have had?"

His soft smile almost dazzles me out of my train of thought. "About a year and a half."

"Have you dated anyone since we started talking online?"

He doesn't answer right away, my heart drops to my stomach. "No. I can tell you honestly, I have not seen anyone since we started talking."

"Bradley, I only know the formula for my stories, I know

nothing about actually dating someone." I shift to lean my head back against the couch.

"Okay, so if this was a story what would the couple be doing right now?" I feel the couch dip as he sits next to me.

"At the two-year mark?" I rub my forehead. "They would either be about to break up from a miscommunication or they would be near a proposal." I sigh. "Now, I am wondering how I have ever sold one book with that kind of logic."

"Move in with me." His tone is serious. I cut my gaze to him. "No."

A frown appears on his perfect face. I feel horrible for being the reason for his unhappiness. "Why?"

"Because I have no interest in ever living in California."

His face lights up a smidge, "Is that the only reason you are saying no?"

I lift my head to really consider this man. "No, but it is the main reason. The other is, I just feel like we need to know more about one another before making such a commitment."

"What if we live together as a trial to see how we like it?" His fishing is adorable. It almost makes me forget that he is trying to get me to agree to something off the wall.

"Isn't that just a pipe dream? Like playing house or something? It is make believe, right?"

"Would you be on your best behavior and not show me exactly who you are?" He raises an eyebrow.

"I don't pretend for anyone." My answer more matter of fact than I intended. "What if you don't like how I behave in public, or how I speak when in the limelight?" I can't help the sigh that comes, "What if..."

"What if no issues come out of us doing a trial living together and you fall madly in love with me?" His smile fades as I let his words wash over me. He waits a few moments before asking, "If we were living together and dating would we be at the sharing a bed stage yet?"

I give him a small smile. "Hmmm, how long of a trial are you thinking?"

CHAPTER 31

BRADLEY

Forever. I want to answer her, but I reign myself in, she hasn't ran from the room screaming. That's a good sign. "How about two weeks?"

Elsie bites her bottom lip as she looks across the room to the blank tv screen that is off. I'm tired, I have no idea what time it is, but I feel like this is going to be the decision that either makes or breaks my entire life. "I am serious. I don't want to live in California. If that is a deal breaker for you, because your entire empire is here, I can understand, but it doesn't change anything."

"You can work literally anywhere," I counter.

Elsie glances at me and abruptly gets up from the couch. "I will compromise on this trial so long as you are forced to come see how I live in my home state."

I get to my feet. "Okay, now that we are on the same page I am going to take my shower." I brush my lips on hers as I turn toward the bathroom.

She follows me, "Sorry, I need my phone." She grabs it and turns to leave. I let her. I make quick work of my shower. I see the black sweatpants, my boxers, and a clean white undershirt on the sink that I didn't place there when I open the shower door. I don't think I have ever gotten dressed so fast in my life. In the ten minutes I was in the shower Elsie hung up her dresses from the shop, hooked my phone up to a charger, and put my items from my overnight bag away. She isn't in her room. I hear her voice softly singing coming from down the hall. Following the sound, I find her in the kitchen. Another odd song is playing through her phone, and she is singing along. Her back to me. She doesn't seem shocked to find me watching her as she turns around, she keeps singing until the song ends.

"I have always wanted to dance in the kitchen." I try to hide how tired I am.

My luck is holding strong as a nice slow love song comes on Elsie's phone. She looks at her phone, I slip my hands around her waist. Once again, as if second nature she puts her arms around my neck. "I've never danced with anyone before," she whispers as she lays her head against my chest.

I fear she will hear how hard my heart is beating. "Never? You haven't been to a school dance or a wedding?" I muse reminding myself that soon I will be able to sleep. She is silent as we continue to sway. Her hair brushes my hands around her waist. As the music ends I release her. Elsie grabs her phone and turns the music off.

"I didn't go to school dances because no one ever asked me." Elsie slowly raises her gaze to mine. "My only friend has always been Mariah." Emotion colors her tone. Elsie blinks rapidly then takes a deep breath. "Ok, I have to..." She looks at me, then glances around the kitchen. "You need to go to bed."

I can't help but chuckle. "Are you sending me to bed?" The idea sounds so good right now. "But I will only go to bed if you do too." I reach out to play with a lock of her hair.

Elsie hesitates. "I can only sleep if the TV is on."

"I can sleep through anything. Are you agreeing to sleeping together?" I release her hair to grab her hand. We walk together to the bedroom.

"We have been together for two years..." she muses. Sleep

suddenly sounds like an awful idea. She lets me lead her to the king-sized bed. I let Elsie's hand slip from mine as she climbs into the bed on the opposite side. She grabs the remote to look at the cable guide on the screen. "Oh! How awesome!" She beams at me, after she picks the channel.

"What are you putting on?" I slide under the blanket.

"*The Godfather* is on. They are playing all three in order. Perfect!" She snuggles against her pillows. Her gaze flits to me. "I have to warn you: I am up and down most of the night." She places her hand under her face. "If it is too much just tell me so I can occupy another space."

I can't help my laugh. "Better than the last time I shared a hotel with my sister. She punched me in her sleep. There was only one queen bedroom when we went on a random vacation a few years ago. I haven't forgiven her." Elsie's face pales a little and she swallows hard. "But if you punch me, I will survive and forgive you." I kiss her nose. She gives a small smile. I roll over to turn off the lights and lay back down.

$\mathcal{E}$LSIE

He is asleep almost as soon as his head hits his pillow. It is almost four in the morning, and it occurs to me that he mentioned staying here for a few days. I reach over to grab my phone. I pull up my trusty grocery app and put in an order. I set my alarm to go off before my order should be delivered, which if I fall asleep now would be about two whole hours.

The last thing I remember before hearing my alarm going off is the car exploding in *The Godfather*. I quiet the alarm and roll over to face Bradley. He is still dead to the world. I resist the urge to touch him. I make my side of the bed after I exit it. My playlist is on low as I brush my teeth. I have to keep reminding myself to keep noise to a minimum because there is someone asleep.

As I take my favorite coffee pods out of the baggie Mariah packed me, I send a silent prayer of thanks to my most favorite person. The coffee maker is heating up as I set up my laptop on the breakfast bar. The hotel phone rings, and I answer before the first trill rings out. "Hello?"

"Yes, I have a grocery carrier here for a Miss Elsie Williams." The woman's voice seems uninterested. She's probably about to go home.

"Can you please send them up?" I try to keep my voice pleasant as I pop the coffee pod into the machine.

"I will send a staff member up. Since you are in the penthouse it is policy not to let anyone up who isn't a registered guest." Her reply is formal.

"Okay, thank you very much." I hang up. With my coffee in hand, I check my phone as I wait by the door for my order. In just two or three minutes there is a soft knock on the door. The tall staff member stands in the doorway and hands me bag after bag. As he hands me the last one, I hand him a twenty-dollar bill for helping me. I close the door and relatch the lock.

Before I work on putting all the items away, I type a message to Mariah telling her that I think she needs to take some time off. I am between book launches so now is the perfect time for her to take the time off and to focus on her and Nate. It is con season, so I really won't have anything fun for her to do while I'm off being in nerd heaven.

Mindlessly I whip up a batch of monkey bread to snack on through the morning. I'm not sure if Bradley likes to eat breakfast or what his preferences are but I can snack on this the next few days if it turns out I'm the only one who likes it. I set the timer for the oven as I place the pan inside. I log into *Annex* and see if anyone needs help and check out my character sale stats for the loot I sold for our clan. I log on to my lower-level character and stake her in front of a major city while I put away all the groceries I got while the bread bakes. My phone's ringtone is loud compared to the quiet morning I was having.

"Hello?" I keep my voice low so I don't disturb Bradley.

"I tried calling Mariah to take care of this latest development, but she told me she was on vacation this week," my publisher laments.

"Yea, I figured Mariah needed a little time to herself." I give myself a mental shake. Talking to Sasha, my publisher of *Death Burns Within*. "So, what do you need to talk about?"

"Preorders have doubled on the newest book from what our

total first year sales were on your first book. I have gotten several calls from many studios wanting to meet with both of us to discuss a miniseries."

The silence drags on, and the oven timer goes off. "Hang on a second." I put down my phone to don an oven mitt to pull out the bread. With a sigh I pick my phone back up and toss the mitt on the counter. "I am not comfortable with selling the rights to make that series into a miniseries."

"How about I send over the offers to your email so you can make sure you don't want to accept?" She sounds hopeful.

I can't help but shake my head. "I know it is that hardest idea for you to understand, but money isn't going to change my mind."

"What would?" She sounds annoyed.

"If I had final say in the outcome, and the ability to participate in the entire process. I don't want them to take my entire world and basterdize it."

"That is a big stipulation." She groans. "I don't think we will be able to find any of them to agree to it."

CHAPTER 33

BRADLEY

It takes me a moment after waking to remember where I am and why. Elsie isn't in the bed; her side of the bed has been remade. I smell cinnamon, and I hear her voice. Her voice gets louder the closer I get to it. I pause listening in the hall.

I hear her sigh. "I can't think of anyone I would consider for writing a script." Her shadow gets smaller as she moves within the kitchen. "Why my series? There are bigger out there to trample on and make a mockery out of." A minute passes. "I'm not trying to be willfully difficult. You knew when you became my agent I don't do anything for the sake of money. I have no interest whatsoever."

I inch closer and see she is typing on her computer. I'm still groggy from the little sleep I got it takes me a second to focus enough to notice she is playing *Annex*. "Sasha, I'm serious. Don't push me."

I see Elsie place her phone on the counter, pushing the speaker button, she turns the volume down a little. "Hold that thought, Sasha." Elsie types furiously on the computer. A chat pops up with a link she clicks on. It connects to her laptop mic, "Okay, you need to make that spell a macro, so that you can

149

spam it when we are in a takedown. Stay out of the voids and run counterclockwise when the mob releases." She mutes her mic.

"Are you seriously playing that fucking lame game while on a call that is literally your sole income?"

"Don't knock the game if you've never played it." Her voice is indignant. "I really don't know why you even wanted to have this meeting; you already knew what I was going to say to making a miniseries."

A miniseries? Depending on who wanted it that could be an insane amount of money. As if the caller had the same thought they say, "Elizabeth, many companies want it. They are willing to outbid each other." Elsie leans on the counter; her hands cover her eyes. "At least check out their pitches."

"If I say yes to reading them over, will it end this conversation?" Elsie sounds defeated.

"For now." The woman on the phone sounds hopeful.

"Done." Elsie goes back to typing on the computer.

"So, how are you and Derrik Derrikson getting along? Have you thought about going to Vegas just to have one of those short marriages of convenience?"

Elsie stops typing. "Absolutely not." She looks over at her phone, her typing forgotten. "In all the years you have known me, you know that I don't do anything I don't want to. I don't sell out. I am true to myself."

"You know that sounds wonderful on paper, but the facts are the facts. Sometimes the ends justify the means." The woman on the phone sounds like she is moving papers around. "So, have you seen the latest tabloids?"

"No. I can't say I have. I find I lack interest when it comes to anything written about me."

The woman clicks her tongue. "You know sometimes you should look to make sure they aren't saying something totally outlandish."

"I pay someone to keep tabs and they deal with the really egregious stories." She gathers her hair and holds it up off her neck. "Why do you mention it now?"

"Because it is being reported you are the granddaughter of Horace Miller." The woman pauses. The name sounds familiar. It's too early for my brain to work. Luckily, I am saved by Elsie.

"That is preposterous. Why did I grow up in foster care if my family owned Miller Productions?"

"They just partnered with Sci Works, so now they are Miller Works Productions."

"Perfect. Let me guess, that is why their lawyer called me yesterday wanting me to give them a sample of my DNA."

"They called you?" The woman sounds excited.

"Well, if you do turn out to be their lost granddaughter, they will expect you to take their last name and marry someone like Derrik." There is a clap on the other end of the phone. "Ugh!" She groans, "And I just said exactly what I shouldn't have." Elsie slams her laptop closed.

"I make my own life. I am not a trained animal. Derrik and I are not up for discussion." She moves her laptop back from her, "From anyone. I am not going to entertain the notion of being in a family that I have never heard of, and I am not going to look at any of those proposals from any company until after con season." Elsie lets her hair back down. "With that in mind you know I am on vacation from today until after Mariah's wedding."

"Your next book goes live in two weeks!" The woman's voice is shrill. Elsie pushes the volume button again to make her voice quieter.

"So? It is a book release not an event." Elsie shakes her head.

"You are a speaker at two of the cons next week."

"You have a point to make? Are you suggesting I can't handle a simple panel event on my own?" Elsie moves to open a cabinet and grabs two plates down.

"Not at all. I was merely reminding." There is some tapping on the other end of the phone. "Is Derrik going with you to the cons?"

"That concludes our meeting. I have notes to type up. Good-bye, Sasha." Elsie hangs up without another word. I watch her move toward the oven to tend to whatever smells delicious. I make sure I am not too quiet as I walk into the kitchen. She is too tempting to not touch. My arms wrap around her middle as I hug her from behind. Her hair is over her other shoulder leaving her neck exposed. I take advantage of her position to hold her close as I trail light kisses down her neck.

"You weren't in bed," I state, keeping my voice low.

"I told you, I have insomnia. That was not an exaggeration." Her own voice is breathless as she tilts her head more to give me better access.

"I smelled something cooking." I nip at her earlobe.

Elsie shivers as she leans her head back on my shoulder. "I made breakfast." She moves to stand straight again. "I wasn't sure if you eat breakfast or what you might like so I got a little of everything."

"A little of everything?" I loosen my grasp on her to turn her to look at me.

Her gaze looks from me to the refrigerator. "I had groceries delivered."

"How long was I out?" I feel like I missed days instead of hours.

"A few hours. I got up around six, but I placed the order before I went to sleep this morning," she admits. Her eyes finally looking up at me.

"You made us breakfast?" She nods before my mouth covers hers. I meant it as a token of thanks, but the chaste kiss changed to passion in a flashpoint of a second. Elsie's silk nightgown slides under my fingers as my hand roams over her body. As quickly as it started it ended. Elsie pulls away enough to stop the contact. Her eyes are still closed.

"Sorry. I'm not sure what came over me." Her tone is soft but husky.

I keep my hold on her. "You know some couples get married within a few months of dating."

She smiles. "But we aren't some couples." She kisses my cheek. She tries to move out of my grasp.

"I want to amend our trial." Elsie's gaze drops to my mouth before looking back into my eyes.

"Okay? I'm listening," she whispers.

CHAPTER 34

$\mathcal{E}$LSIE

I wait for him to speak. My heart beats harder as the seconds carry on.

"Two weeks of trial living together," he states. "And if it goes by without either of us having problems, I suggest we follow through with getting engaged."

I can't help the eyeroll. "You can't be serious." I shake my head with a light laugh. He reluctantly releases me. I pull a big piece of the bread apart and place it on one of the plates I had gotten down. I pull a bite for myself and pop it into my mouth as I turn to hand him his plate. He takes it but uses his other hand to grab my wrist, his tongue connects with my finger. His eyes don't leave mine as he sucks on my finger. He is mesmerizing, and sexy.

He releases my finger and my wrist. He puts his plate down before he cages me against the counter. I can't help the smile that pulls up my lips. "I've written this scene." My whisper sounds breathy.

"I know." He plays with the bottom of a lock of my hair. "I read it." His fingers release my hair to trail down my arm. "I would like to see if we can recreate that scene." He trails his nose along my jaw.

He straightens his head to stare at me. I bite my lower lip trying to stop the new ache my body feels since that first kiss. I can't help the nagging thought that I'm not good enough for this man.

Bradley moves his arms from holding on to the counter on either side of me to wrapping them around me.

CHAPTER 35

BRADLEY

I want to tell her how much I want her. I wasn't kidding when I said I would marry her tomorrow, I can't imagine not having her in my life now that I found her, but my sister's words resurface. 'She isn't one of your trashy girlfriends.'. Natalie is absolutely right; Elsie is so much more.

Elsie's phone rings, breaking the spell we were both falling under. She gives me an apologetic look before she turns to grab her phone. She turns as she hits answer to kiss me, her hand plays with the stubble on my cheek. "Hello?" She says as she takes her lips from mine. Elsie hits the speaker button, places her phone on the counter, then opens a cabinet.

"Elizabeth?" The woman's voice is frail.

"Good morning, Evaline." Elsie looks at the phone for a moment before she moves to the sink to wash up a few of the dishes she used to make breakfast.

"I can put them in the dishwasher," I whisper. She playfully nudges me with her elbow, and she shakes her head.

"I don't use the dishwasher." She looks up at me.

"You wash your own dishes by hand? Every night?"

"Yep, since I was fourteen." She giggles softly.

"How was yesterday?" the old woman inquires.

"Well, it was interesting. I got asked on my first date and I got engaged all in one day." She raises her voice a little to make sure her friend can hear her.

"That sounds like a whirlwind. How do you feel about everything that happened?" There is a slight chuckle on the other side of the phone.

Elsie laughs with her. "I am pleasantly surprised." She turns off the water then starts drying the dishes as I sit at the breakfast bar to eat her amazing breakfast. "This all started as an improv because I was being pursued, but I think he might actually like me." Elsie glances at me as she speaks.

"You sound just like my Sarah."

"Did Sarah have a whirlwind romance too?"

"She was engaged when she died." There is a sniffle from the phone. "We buried her in her wedding dress." Evaline blows her nose. "She was the most beautiful woman."

"I'm so sorry, Evaline." Elsie's eyes tear up before she refocuses on putting away dishes. She's too short to get the mixing bowl into the cabinet. I rush to help her before she gets hurt, but Elsie beats me to it. She puts the large bowl down then hops up on the cabinet to place the bowl in its spot.

"Thank you for talking about my daughter. Today I have to go to physical therapy." Evaline changes the subject.

"How is the weather in Ohio today?" Elsie askes as I come up to stand between her legs. She leans forward to close the cabinet, her gaze locks on mine as she sits straighter on the counter.

"It is sprinkling now, but we are supposed to get thunderstorms later tonight." Evaline coughs. "I love the rain."

"Storms are my favorite. Especially if I can sit on the front porch and read or write during a heavy rain."

"We are of like minds then." You can almost hear the smile on her face. "Would you mind if I call you later?"

"Of course! I enjoy talking to you." Elsie smiles toward the phone. "Talk later, Evaline."

"Goodbye, dear." The woman hangs up. The silence descends over us like a cozy blanket. No sooner had the silence came but Elsie's phone rings again.

"Are you normally this popular?" I joke.

Elsie tenses for a moment, I give her a quizzical look as I answer her phone for her and put it on speaker like she prefers. She gifts me a small smile.

"Hello?" Elsie calls, not taking her eyes off me.

"Don't you 'hello' me! What do you mean I need time off?" Mariah's voice fills the penthouse.

"Mariah, leave her be!" Nate pleads in the background.

"I'm going into con week. You will be bored to tears. This way Nate gets more time with you, and I get to fend for myself."

"You don't have to do this," Mariah whispers, I'm fairly certain she doesn't know she is on speaker or she doesn't know Elsie isn't alone.

"Mariah, I promise I will be okay. Besides, you will need to tell Nate soon, might as well do it before you get married to him. You can't go into a marriage with secrets. I know. I write about it."

"Elizabeth, I'm not sure I'm doing the right thing." Mariah's voice breaks.

"I can't help you make that call. But for what it's worth, I think Nate is perfect for you." Elsie purses her lips.

"Are you doing this to try and get out of the bachelorette party or conveniently miss your flight to make the wedding at the tail end?" Elsie hangs her head slightly, her eyes fixed on the floor. She doesn't speak. "The thought crossed your mind, didn't it?"

"Yes," Elsie whispers. I don't think anyone could have heard her.

Mariah groans, "Elizabeth, you're my maid of honor. You can't leave me all alone there." Mariah reasons. "Maybe you can bring Derrik, so you at least have someone in your corner if I'm not able to be by your side the whole night." Elsie turns her head away from the phone, a lone tear rolling down her cheek. "Elsie, is Derrik with you right now? Am I on speaker?"

Elsie whispers one more, "Yes."

"Derrik, can you pick up the phone and take it off speaker?" Mariah asks. Elsie doesn't try to stop me. Emotions are playing across her face. Sadness is the main emotion I can see. I tentatively grab Elsie's phone and take it off speaker.

"Hello." I keep my eyes on Elsie.

"Good morning. I'm sure you haven't had much sleep knowing Elsie."

"I slept fine." I know my face registers I have no idea how to take that comment. "What can I do for you?"

"Would you be able to attend our wedding? It is in three days." Mariah waits for my answer.

"I would be honored to attend your wedding."

"I need your number to get ahold of you later. There are some things you need to know if you are serious about Elizabeth." Mariah's voice is low.

"Sure, let me just text it to you now." I kiss Elsie's cheek.

"Thanks, talk to you soon." Mariah hangs up. I text Mariah my number from Elsie's phone before I set it on the counter. "What would you like to do today?" My question seems to catch her off guard. She opens her mouth to speak but instead her phone rings. She sighs as she reaches for it and looks at the screen before answering. "Hello?"

This time she doesn't place the phone on speaker. Elsie tilts her head back and closes her eyes, I can't help but take the opportunity to kiss her neck. "Yes, I can attend a conference call, is it possible to give me about fifteen minutes to gather my notes and get my laptop out?" There is a moment before Elsie continues. "Thank you, talk in just a few." She hangs up, her hands touch my face. She moves her lips to mine. Her initiating a real kiss is doing things to my body. Our kiss doesn't last long enough. "Bradley. I have to have a conference call for the con I am going to on Friday." I press my mouth to hers again murmuring an "mmhmm" against her lips. She sighs as she lets me deepen the kiss. "Please," I hear her whisper. I pull away to look at her. Her face is flushed, her hands are still on my face, her eyes are closed, and her lips curve up in a soft smile.

"I promise to be back as soon as I can." She finally looks up at me.

"Where are you going?" I nuzzle her neck her voice when she speaks tickles my nose.

"I am going to go into the spare bedroom, if that is okay with you." She pauses. "Or if you prefer, I can find a meeting room in the hotel to use."

"I never want you to leave our space." I pull away from her finally to let her down from the counter. I watch her gather her laptop and take her phone with her into the bedroom across from the one we shared last night. As soon as she closes the door, I hear my own phone go off. I rush to answer it.

"Hello?" I answer with annoyance.

"Hey, it's Mariah, is Elsie on her conference call?"

"Yes, how do you know that she was on one?" I glance at the closed door where Elsie is.

"I'm her PA, I know her schedule like the back of my hand. I set all this up. Since she put me on vacation, I totally forgot to give her the itinerary."

Here is my chance to ask a few questions. "Why does Elsie need a date for your wedding? Don't get me wrong, I am excited to have any reason to go anywhere with her, but it sounded like she would be alone for the whole night."

Mariah sighs. "I know you don't know much about Elsie's personal life, so I am going to give you a quick overview because I think you really care for her and I don't want her hurt because she hates talking about herself, typically."

"So, I am finding." I can't help the chuckle that comes out..

"Elsie came to live with my family when she was thirteen. When she aged out of foster care she still came to our house for dinners and my parents adored her. She didn't want to be adopted, it was her wishes, we respected her decision. It was the only decision she could make for herself. When my parents died they split everything between me, my two brothers, and Elsie. My entire family thinks she is a drain on the family and a disgusting human for attaching herself to my parents. Elsie pays me to manage her entire life. I don't have much to do because Elsie takes care of most things on her own. After college I had the hardest time finding a job and helping my parents when they got sick." Mariah blows her nose. "She literally funds my entire life, but she didn't want anyone to know." Mariah pauses. "No, that is a lie. I didn't want anyone to know that I spent so much time and money in college only to never use my degree. Another reason my family looks down on Elsie is she never went to college; she was a hit from the start but none of them know how big she has made it. If you come to the wedding, you might see an Elsie you don't recognize or maybe one you can't respect. When she comes around my family, she goes into survival mode." She hiccups. "She is quiet, and reclusive. She doesn't want confrontation because she doesn't want to reveal my secrets to them." Mariah sighs. "It is one of the reasons Nate has a problem with her. My family is poison to her character."

"I'll be Elsie's date." I reconfirm.

"One thing I need you to know. You can't call her Elsie at the wedding."

"Why?"

"It was my parent's nickname for her, and my family will be relentless, even at a wedding, over her using it after their deaths and making money under it," Mariah explains.

"Ok, so what is her name when around your family?"

"Elizabeth Lucus. Her legal name." Mariah hesitates a second. "You do like her, don't you?"

"Very much," I answer. "Got any pointers?"

"Always be honest. If you ever lie to her and she finds out..."

"She'll kill me?" I tease.

Mariah is silent for a moment. "Worse. She will disappear."

"Excuse me?" I try to cover the thrill of laughter I feel for that odd turn of conversation.

"That is how she became Elsie Williams. She let a guy close when she was seventeen or eighteen. He used her. He is one of my brother's best friends. They poisoned him against her. She stopped going to events and withdrew from everyone until she was ready, but she never came back home."

Vaguely I remember my sister mentioning that Elsie disappeared from everything, but I thought she said it was because of family trying to claim they were related or tried suing her... I can't remember now. "Got it. Anything else?"

"Caffeine is your friend if you want to keep up with her." Mariah giggles. "But if you ever make her mad, Oreos are your lifesaver."

"Good to know." I laugh.

"Oh! If you want to have a romantic night. Elsie doesn't usually drink alcohol. But if you are securely home, she might indulge in some wine, sweet wine only. I better go before Nate comes looking for me." Mariah exhales hard. "Elsie is right, I need to tell Nate everything."

"Talk to you later." Mariah hangs up first.

I look through the cabinets and refrigerator to see what I can whip up for lunch. It takes very little time to whip up some spaghetti and seasoned meat. I don't want to bother Elsie while she is in a meeting but I do plate her some before I decide to lay on the couch and catnap while I wait. I must have really dozed off because when I finally do wake up it is dark outside, and the smell of garlic and onions are in the air. As I lay here, I notice the curtains have been closed and there is a blanket pulled over me. I fall a little more in love with this woman every minute. I hear an alarm going off, then I hear her in the kitchen again.

"One sec, I will be right back, don't pull that group of zombies until I am back." She opens a cabinet and the fridge before I finally hear her speak again. "Okay, Dreexir, pull that group when it walks in front of you again. Zhirix, you need to toss your army to passive and mass attack the smaller enemies." The clicks from her keyboard are loud in the silent space. "Very good.

Perfect, now pop those advances and if you have an army ready to fight send them now." Another minute then more silence. "Congratulations guys. Now you all have your titles for end game content." Holy shit did she really just lead an entire take down for current end game for our clan? My heart swells with pride. Memories from our first meeting come to mind. She lead the clan to end game content back then too. "Okay, give me one sec, I have another timer going off and then I can get on my other character and help you do some of that content." I hear her set something down.

Her footsteps are soft as she makes her way to me. "Sorry, I didn't want to wake you. I know you didn't sleep much last night." She runs her fingers through my hair. "I made lasagna and garlic bread if you are hungry."

"You made us dinner?" I move to sit up.

She steps back from me with a worried look on her face as she plays with the fake wedding set on her left hand. "Would you have preferred to go out? Do you want me to..." I stand quickly silencing her with my mouth.

"It sounds amazing," I reassure her. She relaxes as she pulls away from me.

CHAPTER 36

Elsie

I bend to grab the blanket off the couch I had used to cover him. Bradley watches me as I fold it. "Why are you staring at me?" I don't look at him as I finish my task. I hear my phone ringing. I reach to grab it out of my back pocket. "Hello?"

"I hope you find a reason not to come to our sister's wedding; you know you aren't welcome here." Daniel's voice is full of hate. Part of me wishes he was drunk, but I know how much the family really hates me. He hangs up without waiting for a reply. My brain goes into overdrive. What if the honeymoon phase ends and gives way to resentment, or what if one of Mariah's brothers get in Bradley's ear and turn him against me too? My stomach lurches at the thought of Bradley looking at me like the rest of Mariah's family does.

"Are you okay? Honey?" Hmm, that sounds natural coming out of his mouth. "Else? Maybe I should call you Lizzy." That gets my full attention. "You look like you just saw a ghost." The concern is etched in his beautiful face, his brow has worry lines and his eyes are sharp as he steps closer.

"I think it would be a good idea to maybe play the twenty

questions you suggested a few days ago." Might as well get some truths spoken before I fall too far.

Bradley gives me the most dazzling smile I have seen. "Okay!"

"Let's sit on the couches and talk," I suggest. I move to go collect two plates of food so we can eat while we talk. Before I return to where he is sitting I send a message to my group that I had something come up, then I turned off my laptop.

I hand him his plate. He takes one couch and I take the other. The coffee table becomes the ocean between our private islands.

"What would you like to know?" he prods, as he takes a bite of lasagna.

"Before we start asking questions, what has Mariah told you?" I trust my sister, but I need to see his emotions on his face when he repeats what she told him.

"She gave me some pointers." He isn't lying but he is not telling the whole truth. I know Mariah; she spilled more than just pointers.

"And what else did she tell you?" My left brow lifts as I inquire.

"She told me that if you ever feel wronged you can make yourself disappear." He pulls a piece of bread to pop in his mouth, he chews and studies me. He finishes his bite. "What does that mean exactly?"

I can't help the frown at the mention of my great lesson on pseudo love. I take a deep breath. "Once upon a time," I try to manage a small smile, but I just don't have the energy, "there was a young, dumb girl who was so lonely she wrote stories to escape. Stories where she was loved and known. Where she had friends and could do all kinds of amazing things." I look up at a spot on the opposite wall, as if I could see the past playing on the surface. "Mariah's parents wanted to adopt me, but as much as they loved me, Mariah's brothers tormented me. They pretended in front of their parents and Mariah, but when they weren't around, Daniel and Marcus made me feel worthless. I wasn't a person to them. But one summer, Daniel's best friend came to stay for a month.

Colin spoke to me like I mattered. He paid attention to me." I don't realize I am crying until Bradley wipes the tears off my face. I close my eyes as I finish the story. Taking strength from the man in front of me I continue. "Mariah's parents went for a weekend away. I had just turned eighteen; Mariah is their youngest and she was nineteen. So, it was fine to leave us alone. Her brothers bought alcohol and threw a low-key party. It was the first and last time I ever drank. Colin convinced me that he wanted to be with me. That I was who he wanted." My gaze finds Bradley. "Alcohol makes all the words sound honest." I grab a lock of my hair. "I let him get too close. I didn't use common sense."

"What made you see the truth?" he asks, and even though his voice is soft, his words drop like bombs in my head.

"The next day I overheard him bragging to Daniel about being with me. Then Daniel ridiculed Colin for sinking so low to need to fuck the family pet." I can't help the scowl. "Colin didn't like being the punchline, so he joined them in their treatment of me. I packed my life into two bags and left. Mariah's parents called when they got home, and I just told them I had gotten a job offer for writing and needed to start as soon as humanly possible."

"Did you ever tell anyone what really happened?" His hand traces circles on my back.

"I told Mariah. And I was never sorrier for speaking the truth in my entire life."

His brow furrows. "Sorry for telling your only friend what was going on?"

"Those are her family. I know Mariah and I have a special relationship, but it wasn't fair of me to unburden myself on her like that." I purse my lips. "So, I started going by my penname and haven't been back."

"You haven't been back to visit at all?"

"No, Mariah's parents would visit me." I dab at my tears. "When they got too sick to travel I video called them every night. I hired nurses to care for them. Mariah had just graduated, and she was so overwhelmed. But if I had shown up then, it would have caused too much stress on Mariah and her parents. So, I stayed away.

"When they died, I asked Mariah to work for me. Making her life a little easier makes me happy."

"What happens when she has her own kids or wants to move away from your area?" His questions are valid.

"Mariah can work from anywhere, at any time, or for as long as she wants to." My smile is genuine and automatic as I think of my friend. "I'd do anything for Mariah. She is the only human who has not been turned against me."

"That is all it takes to earn your undying loyalty?" Bradley attempts to joke.

I avoid his scrutiny by moving food around on my plate. "She's the only person who ever treated me like I mattered."

"I *know* you matter." His tone is hard, his emphasis on know is unmistakable. I chance looking at him. I have written about men looking at the leading lady with adoration or conviction, I have never experienced such a circumstance, until this moment. "I also *know* that I love you."

My breathing ceases. I hold it waiting for the punchline, or the other shoe to drop. No one is this perfect.

"Are you waiting for me to return the sentiment?" I whisper as I finally let myself resume breathing.

He smirks as he tucks my hair behind my ear. "Only when it is true."

"When?"

"Make no mistake, honey, I'm in this for the long haul." Bradley's fingers trace my jaw.

"What is your favorite color?" My question comes out more of a whisper than I intended.

Bradley grins, it makes his eyes sparkle. His gaze sweeps over me. "Black."

"Black is not a color; it is a shade." Inwardly I cringe over my need to spout factoids at stupid times.

"You do like to give out the most random facts." He laughs.

"Actually, I think I owe you all the credit for every bit of useless information you have told the clan in the last couple of years I have retained."

I elbow him. "Answer the question."

Bradley's smile widens. "My favorite color used to be green, but now it is limestone gray."

CHAPTER 37

BRADLEY

Her confusion lasts only a moment, her eyes widen a little before she bursts into a fit of giggles. Elsie is the most beautiful woman I have ever seen, and when she is happy there is no competition on this planet.

"Are you telling me my eye color is now your favorite over green?" I nod, then she continues, "I used to get made fun of because of how light and clear they are."

Made fun of? Elsie? She's ethereal. "Kids are cruel," is all I can think to say. I mull over my next question, but I'm worried it will count as one of the allocated. "Else," I begin.

She gives me another odd look. "I have never had anyone use a nickname that wasn't family."

"Do you want me to stop?" Maybe she isn't into nicknames.

"'Else is different," she tilts her head, "I feel like you're about to say, *or else*."

"I also like to call you honey." Elsie's blush is instant. "What about Lizzy?"

Elsie purses her lips for a moment as she considers the pet name. "It is okay, as long as only you call me that." She closes her eyes for a moment then opens them to lock on me. "I will never call you, Brad."

My turn to give her a quizzical look. "Okay, thank you for that, but why?"

"Because Brad does not sound right when speaking to you or about you." She shrugs. Elsie gives a shy smile, I grab her hand to fold our fingers together. "What if I decided on a pet name for you?"

"Honey, you can call me anything as long as we are together." I bring her hand to my lips to place a soft kiss on the top.

"I'll keep that in mind." We finish our meals in silence. Her face a myriad of emotions. I wait for her to sort her thoughts out. "What is the sexiest thing to you but is mundane to most others?"

Her question makes me think. I used to be with self-centered women. Their makeup was heavy and flawless, their clothes chosen to get the most attention, and their conversation on the shallow end of things. With Elsie I notice more. "I think it is insanely sexy that you play videogames. How you know the lore and characters inside and out." I smile at her. "My stomach flips when you laugh. I love when you play with your hair when you are nervous." I comb my own fingers through her long waves. She blushes a little deeper with each answer. "What mundane things make you hot?"

She takes a deep breath. "I am a sucker for a man who can dress down with seemingly little effort." She giggles. "I also am pleased to discover I love when a man asserts himself, especially when it comes to rescuing me." Elsie reaches out to place her hand on my cheek. "I also think it is sexy that you read my work." She brings her lips to mine. I know I will forget to tell her I think it is sexy when she initiates anything with me, my mind is already gone to the demanding lips of this woman who I would move the stars for.

We make out for what seems like ages. It has been quite a few years since I only made out. Elsie finally gets her fill and pulls away to catch her breath. I brush her hair way from her face, "Would you like a personal tour of *Annex*'s headquarters tomorrow or maybe the next day?" I caress her jaw with my thumb.

"We can do that?" Her voice is no louder than a husky whisper.

I can't help the chuckle. "We can do anything. Else. I own it."

Her smile is infectious. "Yes, please." She grabs her hair to play with a lock.

I put my hand over hers. "What is it, Else?"

"Could we watch my favorite Disney princess tonight?" Her eyes are big and pleading. "If you fall asleep that's okay, but I did tell you I would subject you to it." She gives me a small hopeful smile.

"Sure, honey. We can watch whatever makes you happiest," I assure her.

Elsie kisses my cheek before she gathers our plates and moves to take them in the kitchen.

*E*LSIE

I was only gone for a moment to grab my computer but when I came back into the living room Bradley had made popcorn and the cushions were off the couch and on the floor with all the blankets in the penthouse ready. He had moved the couches and coffee table to make the living room into our own little movie in the park vibe.

"Is this, okay?" His uncertainty is endearing. I fall a little more in love with him.

I reach up on my tiptoes to give him a peck on the cheek. "This is perfect."

We sat down and got comfortable amongst the pillows and blankets. Our own little nest of comfort. Bradley plugged in my laptop while I found *Enchanted* to watch. Within fifteen minutes of the movie being on and the lights being out the man next to me was out cold. His arm was firmly around me, despite my computer being in my lap.

As soon as my favorite movie is over I check on Bradley. As much as I hate to do it I move his arm off of me so I can get more comfortable while I log in to my game. I check on the clan and see no one online that needs my help. I open my emails and look over the proposals for the mini series and quickly make a few notes and send them back to my agent. I don't say no right off the bat, but I do have several big stipulations and hard boundaries, I am sure this will ultimately be a no.

I catch my gaze fixed on the man laying on the sea of cushions he scattered to watch my movie with me. I think of how my life has changed in the last few days since this man decided he wanted to get to know me more. I wish I could trust my own feelings more and my judgement. Is this what love feels like? I almost resist the urge to caress his sweet face, his cheek is so warm. My touch doesn't wake him but he does turn to press his lips on my palm before he settles back into sleep. I feel the smile stretch my lips. I hope this is how love feels like. I move to cover him with a blanket as I remember a question Bradley and Mariah have both asked me: If I have ever written my own happily ever after. Life truly does imitate art for a lot of my stories why would my own experience be any different? With so many ideas rushing into my mind I stand and grab my laptop as I rush to the spare bedroom. As I open my notepad for notes and start my music up my mind notes the time on my computer, it's

I don't know how long I was writing for, but the sky was bright. Bradley's voice carried down the hall as he spoke to people on Annex. It takes me only moments to alt tab and login.

THORANTIK: I didn't want to disturb you while you were working.

CYBIRA: I get lost in my own stories, sometimes I need help making my way back to civilization.

THORANTIK: I will keep that in mind next time. What did you write about? I have no idea how long you have been in there but I got up around nine AM. . I made you lunch a while ago but decided to leave you in peace. Are you hungry now?

CYBIRA: now that you mention it, I am hungry. I'm working on a standalone. I can take a break for now. Would you like me to make something for dinner?

THORANTIK: I got everything covered if you want to log off and meet me in the living room.

CYBIRA: be right there

With that I log off and hurry out of the room.

CHAPTER 39

BRADLEY

I wait for Elsie in the kitchen. She moves to stand across from me, her hands resting on the island between us. I thread my fingers through hers as we stand there, "Else, have you eaten at all?". She tries to pull her hand from mine, but I don't let it go.

"Don't worry, as you can see I never miss a meal." She attempts to joke. "I eat when I'm hungry."

I make her a plate of the spaghetti I made us for yesterdays lunch that she didn't get to.

"Have some late lunch with me. We can just hang out today." I pull her off a hefty portion of the garlic bread. "Would you like to go swimming after we eat?" I hand her the plate I prepared.

Elsie smiles as she takes it. "Sure." She rips of bite off to eat. We finish eating in comfortable silence. "Would you like some coffee?"

"Actually, that sounds really good." I watch as she flits around the kitchen to make us each a cup. She takes a sip after handing me a hot mug.

"How many cups of coffee have you had this today?" I take a

tentative sip. That small sip has me trying not to choke. This is the most bitter coffee I have ever had.

Elsie covers her laugh with another drink. "This is my third cup," she admits as she finishes her coffee. "Guess I will be getting out of my nightgown after all." She stands to leave the kitchen.

"Well, if this was a traditional relationship you wouldn't have left the bedroom with anything on." I can't help the smirk. I watch her close to see if I pushed too far.

"Aren't you coming to change, so we can go swim?" She turns toward the bedroom we are sharing.

"Don't tease me like that, Else. It makes my mind go to the gutter," I say as I follow her, giving her distance in case she is joking. I'm praying to everything in the world that she is serious. "Though if you do want to go swimming at all you should be careful what you say."

She turns to look up at me as she gets closer to the bed. "Why?"

"Because a woman like you should be loved, valued, and worshipped for hours." As I finish my answer, I barely have time to think before Elsie slowly wraps her arms around my neck. Her gaze intense as she pulls me down to her lips.

"What are you doin', honey?" I move to kiss her cheek.

"Would you like me less if I wanted to..." She trails off like she can't bring herself to speak the words.

I pull back to assess her. With conviction in my voice I say, "I would love you if you didn't want to do anything. I would love you if you wanted everything." I use my fingers to brush her hair away from her face. "But I only want you to do what you want. I'd wait ten lifetimes to be with you."

"I want you," she whispers.

Mentally I remind myself that I need to make this experience amazing and show her how perfect we can be together. While I give myself a silent pep talk Elsie moves to the edge of the bed, my mouth goes dry as I watch her slide the thin black straps of her gown off her shoulders. The silk slips down her skin revealing her body in its wake. Elsie bites her bottom lip and looks at me through her lashes, her gown now pools at her feet.

"Else, you're beautiful." My voice is thick, I wrap one arm around her waist while I bury my other in her long black hair. The passion that flows naturally when we kiss still present as our mouths come together. Neither of us is the winner, but we also can't lose on this point either. Carefully I use my body to lay her on the bed, trying to keep the pace of our kiss in the process. I feel Elsie pull on my shirt. I break our kiss only long enough to take off my shirt. I consider taking off my pants and boxers, I glance at Elsie to see she has moved to lay against the pillows on the bed. I take the extra few seconds to discard all my clothes. Elsie gifts me a sexy smile as she watches me.

Elsie laying against the pillows gives me a chance to look at everything she is. She isn't skinny, but she's perfection.

"I've never let anyone see me naked," she whispers shyly. "I was too scared my only time." Elsie puts her arms over her eyes. The movement lifts her breasts, exposing some black ink.

On instinct I reach out to hold her breast, I hear her quick intake of breath. Elsie arches slightly, pushing more of herself into my hand. I kneel between her legs before I reach for her arms. "Why are you hiding?" I softly tease.

"I am afraid to see the disappointment on your face." Her honesty is refreshing but it reminds me that she has demons.

"Baby, look at me." I lean close to her face and wait for her to comply. As I wait, I shift my knee in between her legs touching her thin silk panties. She lets out a soft moan before she tentatively looks at me.

CHAPTER 40

$\mathcal{E}$LSIE

All of his words warm my heart, I consider him for a moment. That is all it takes to decide that taking this step is worth the risk to make sure all bases are covered should we decide to keep going in this relationship. I would hate to get head over heels and then find there is no passion in the bedroom.

My body is on fire, and he hasn't even touched me yet. What if I look at him and I see how disappointed he is in seeing me naked? Reluctantly I open my eyes. Bradley's face is only inches from mine.

"Do you want me to stop?" I can hear the restraint in his voice.

"Why? Have you changed your mind?" I love how honest I can be with him.

He doesn't use words to answer me. Bradley starts at my lips and slowly kisses his way down my body. He glances up at me before he yanks hard at the silk scrap of fabric that proves to be a weak barricade for him. I hear them rip and feel the cool air touch my skin. Bradley moves my legs, one to the side and one on his shoulder before he places a kiss on my most sensitive part. I can't keep my eyes open, I let myself just feel.

I have no idea what he is doing to me or how he knows what to do, but I lose track of time as I feel pressure build. I'm almost scared, "Let go, baby, I got you." I hear Bradley. He moves his mouth and applies his fingers; my body explodes in response.

When I open my eyes again Bradley is kissing his way back up my body. He licks and sucks on my nipple as his hand massages the other. He moves his hips to take position at my entrance. His gaze locks on mine before he slowly pushes inside me. I rake my fingers through his hair. Bradley's lips capture mine as he sheaths himself in me. He stills his body but deepens the kiss. I take a page out of my own writing and wrap my legs around his waist, "Bradley, please."

He looks at me. "What baby?" His voice is deep.

"Please, move." I pull him back down to get his mouth back on me. Bradley pulls almost completely out before slamming back in. The bite of pain adds to the full feeling. He keeps pace but moves to kiss my neck.

"Elsie..." He groans. I hold on to his shoulders.

"Bradley." His name is a whispered benediction. "I love you." I speak my heart.

He kisses me with fervor. I feel the familiar pressure build, and I hold Bradley tight as I let myself go.

CHAPTER 41

BRADLEY

I feel Elsie's nails dig into my shoulders as her orgasm rolls through her. Her release triggers mine. I stay inside her, because my body doesn't want to move any more than hers wants to let me go. I reach over to pull the blanket over us.

"I love you, Elsie." My tone is low, my lips at her throat.

She giggles. "That tickles."

I move my head to look down at her, "What tickles?" I trail my nose from her collar bone to her ear. Her body shivers.

"Your lips on my throat while you talk." She traces my face with her fingers.

"Did you mean it?" I resist closing my eyes as she plays with my hair.

She arches one of her perfect brows at me. "I don't have a reason to lie to you." She raises up to press her lips to mine. In a quick kiss. "I love what we have had for two years, and I love what we have going on now."

"Mmm," I agree, as I nuzzle her neck. Her legs are still around my waist. I feel my body react to her still being hot and waiting. "I could do this all day with you." Her laugh doesn't help my situation. It's husky and sexy.

"How about we do it when the mood strikes." She scratches my stubble on my face. "In the meantime..." She pauses. I look at her. She is more beautiful than any woman I have ever seen. I carefully pull out of her, she winces. "Could we..."

I lay next to her in the bed. "We can do anything you want, honey." I caress her arm.

"I feel tired." She looks a little confused, but softly chuckles. "It is an odd feeling." She leans over to kiss my neck, like I had done to her.

"If you keep that up, I will have to tire you out more before letting you rest now." She immediately stops, and she blushes as she looks away.

"Hey." I brush her hair out of her face. "How about we relax to some TV and go swimming later?"

"You'll stay with me?" Her tone betrays her emotion.

"I'll always stay. Until you tell me to leave." She turns to lay on her back as she studies me.

Her ink under her breast again peeks out as she moves. I reach over and move her body so I can check out her ink. "Is this your only tattoo?"

She blushes. "Yes."

Sois gentil et tiens courage

"What does it mean?" I trace the words.

"It is French for 'be kind and have courage'." She watches me. "It is the inscription on the inside of Anne Frank's diary."

I release her. "Do you mind if I hold you while we rest?"

She smiles before she turns so her back is to my chest. I wrap my arm around her as she flips the TV on to a movie channel. We both fall asleep watching some movie about crashing a wedding and stealing the bride.

I wake on my back, Elsie's mouth swallowing me. Holy hell it's the hottest thing I have ever seen in my life. I have to tune out the part of my brain that wonders where she learned her skills. "Else, you don't have to do this."

"Shhh, just let me love you," she commands before taking me

back in her mouth. Her hand grips my base and works in tandem at a steady pace. I feel myself getting close before her hand leaves me. Elsie takes all of me down her throat, she lets out a moan that vibrates down my shaft.

"Elsie, I'm gonna..." I try to give her warning. She takes me, tightening her throat as she swallows. I can't stop my orgasm as it shoots through me. I come back to earth; Elsie is using her tongue to lick me clean. She catches me watching her.

She gives me a shy smile. "I've always read about women doing that and always wanted to."

"I don't know what I did to deserve you, but I am so grateful for my luck." I play with a long lock of her hair, "What other things have you read about that you want to try?"

$\mathcal{E}$LSIE

I can't help the blush that comes. "That is the only one that comes to mind."

"I guess I need to read more romance books," he muses. "Come back up here, I like when you're close to me."

I bring the blanket with me as I lay next to him in the bed. I have no idea how long we were out, but I feel full of energy. "I guess I should get up."

"Would you like to take a shower with me?" He sounds like he is still sleepy.

"You can sleep a little longer. I'll take a quick shower then make us something to eat." I play with his scruff on his face as I speak. "I'll come get you when the food is ready."

"Mmm, but sleep sounds boring when you aren't with me." His eyes open before he moves to give me a hard, demanding kiss. "I'll take a shower with you," he whispers against my mouth.

My lips curl into a smile as we make out. My inexperience doesn't seem to matter to him, if anything it spurs him on. His mouth is relentless, his hands hold me close. I hear the moan that escapes my mouth and feel the effect I have on Bradley. It's a heady feeling knowing I incite such responses from such a man.

With reluctance I pull away, "I'm taking my shower now." He lets me disengage from him.

I move to the closet to pull out one of the dresses Bradley bought me from yesterday and to find my bathing suit so I can put it on underneath. I don't feel awkward walking around naked. As I make my way to the bathroom, I grab one of my clips to keep all my hair up and dry while I shower. Since I will have to shower after we swim, I might as well not bother washing my hair now.

I start the water and step into the warm spray. The cold air hits me as Bradley opens the shower door to join me. "My sister warned me not to try to sleep with you, or you'd leave." He grabs the loofah from me to take over the task of washing my arms. "Was she right?"

I tilt my head to look up at him. "Are you just using me for sex?" I feel like I should know the answer, but my track record isn't the best at reading men.

"No." He looks down at me, his gaze is fierce. "I want so much more with you."

I try to hide my smile as he resumes washing me. "What would you like for lunch?"

"It might be a little too late for lunch, honey." He rests his hand on my hip when he finishes his task.

I reach out for the loofah. "Your turn." His smile is sexy. I reach up and stroke his stubble with my thumb. "I like this."

"If you prefer me not to shave, I can do that." He leans down to brush his lips on mine. "So, can we resume our questions?"

"What would you like to know now?" I roll my eyes playfully as I move on to washing his chest.

"What kind of wedding do you want?"

"I don't want a wedding." I was never the type of girl to pretend to have a wedding or a groom. "If I did decide to ever get married, I would just go to the courthouse."

"Even if you had unlimited resources or money at your disposal?"

His follow up question reminds me that money could become a problem with us. I nod. "I make a reasonable living," I glance at him before I move the luffa to his stomach, "but I live a quiet life."

"Is quiet your way of saying you don't spend money?" He takes a quick intake of breath as my hand moves to apply soap to his manhood. I spend a minute or two making sure he is clean before I move to let the water hit him, rinsing the lather from his body.

"I spend money." I huff as I turn off the water. "But I don't waste money."

"So, you wouldn't have booked the penthouse?" He arches a dark brow at me.

I think of it before I grab a towel. "No, not for myself." I carefully dry off as I think of how I want to answer him. "I love to buy things for other people, I like spending money on things that make me happy like my favorite books, or my computer, or my hobbies. But I don't like wasting money on myself when there are simpler ways to achieve the basics that I require."

"Fair enough."

"I don't need anyone to waste their money on me either," I add.

"You are worth more than you realize."

I decide to not argue. He would understand once he gets around Mariah's family. He leaves the bathroom to get dressed. I take the opportunity to toss my suit on and don my dress. As I finish brushing my teeth Bradley comes behind me to wrap his arms around my middle. His stubble on my neck, as he kisses me, sends a shiver down my body. "You're beautiful, Else."

I put my toothbrush into the holder and hold his gaze in the mirror. I watch his hand reach up and unclip my hair. As it cascades down my back, he buries his nose in it. I feel him inhale. "I love you."

My heart melts, I turn to stare up at him. "I love you. I want this to work, more than you could ever know. More than I care to admit."

"I only have one thing that could be a relationship killer." His voice sounds strained, like he is really worried about what he is about to ask.

"Ok," I prepare my heart, "what?"

"Do you want kids?" His eyes rove my face.

"Of my own?" I search his eyes. "What if I can't give you your own children?"

"Are you open to adoption if we can't have our own?" His voice has a thread of hope.

I place both of my hand of his face. "I have never imagined having any. Because I couldn't imagine being a single mother." I lift my body on my tip toes to place a soft kiss on his lips. "But if I did find someone, I would do anything to make them happy."

"That wasn't my question." He fixes me with a hard stare, "I asked if you wanted children."

CHAPTER 43

BRADLEY

Elsie looks at me, and tears brim her eyes. "Yes," she whispers before settling back on the bottoms of her feet.

"Then the rest is just details, my love." I pull her to me, not willing to let her go.

"Those details add up and will matter sooner or later, Bradley." She sighs as she rests her forehead to my chest. "What will become of me when this dream ends?"

"It doesn't ever have to end."

She takes a deep breath before she moves out of my arms, "What do you want for dinner?"

I follow her down the hall to the kitchen noting that it is after seven in the evening. We slept most of the day away. I'm sure Elsie needed to finally sleep for longer than a couple of hours.

"Why don't we order some room service poolside?" I suggest.

Her face lights up. "Can we do that?"

"We can do anything you want." I reach for the hotel phone. "What do you want to eat?"

She grabs the menu off the coffee bar and looks it over. She nibbles on her index nail as she looks over the options. "Do you want to share a pizza?"

"I might eat a piece or two, but I would rather have a burger." Her eyes go back to the menu. She looks distressed but she is making an effort to stifle the panic. Like last night at the signing, the light in her eyes dim. I move to pull her in my arms. "I got you, honey." I tighten my hold on her. She is taking two breaths to each of mine. I stroke her hair. "Breathe with me, Else." She lets out a soft whine as she makes an effort to mimic me. Her nails once again dig into my shoulders, except this time I have a shirt on. I try to reign in my thoughts. "Shhhhh. You're okay. I won't let anything happen to you." I kiss the top of her head. "Do you want me to get you a Xanax?" I keep my voice low.

She shakes her head no. I feel her breathing slowly start to return to normal. "Keep talking." She takes another strained breath. "I hate taking Xanax if I don't have to," she quickly explains.

"Okay." I don't know what to talk to her about. So, I talk about the only thing I could talk about for hours. "Do you remember the first complete take down we were in together?" I don't wait for her to answer. "You led the group of newer players. I was pretending to be one. You knew everyone's make and spell build." I keep my voice even; Elsie still isn't out of the woods. "You walked us through every step. I was amazed with your patience and your knowledge." I chuckle. "You even knew the lore of the clan we were taking over." I look down to look at her. She tilts her head back a little. "Your insight and intuition on how those eighteen other people needed to be directed was astounding."

Her smile is fragile. "You kept doing the opposite of what I told you to do." She takes an almost normal breath. "I thought you just hated having a woman tell you what to do."

"I just wanted to see if I could get you mad." I can't help but think of another question for her. "What kind of temper do you have?"

I love how Elsie's emotions always show on her face. It is nice that she doesn't try to hide who she is. She doesn't seem to care who I am at all.

"My temper is absolute. When it is in full swing, I run. The only person to ever get me to the point of anger is Mariah." She shrugs. "Nate can get me to raise my voice though." She admits. "When I get mad at Mariah, I binge horror movies and avoid her for a little while. If I am in the wrong, I make her a new blanket or wreath, and if Mariah is in the wrong, she..."

"Brings you Oreos?" I finish.

She narrows her eyes and smirks a little. "I see she has given you advice on how to get out of trouble with me."

"I think I could find something a little better than sandwich cookies to make you happy again," I whisper in her ear.

She pulls away, the blush instant, "Let's order so we can go swim. I would like a bacon pizza, please."

"So polite." I watch as she opens the fridge. I place the order and instruct them to bring it to the pool. I add a chilled bottle of wine to be put in our room while we are out as well.

"What kind of temper do you have?" Elsie closes the fridge, two cans of Coke in her hands. She walks to me, one hand extended to offer me a soda.

I take it using the extra moments to word my answer. "My temper?" I repeat, "My temper used to be quick and physical. I used to get into fights with guys in school so often. Now, that I am older and wiser?" I wink at Elsie, "I tend to use forethought to thwart people before they can strike me first."

Elsie studies me as she opens her can of soda. My gaze travels from her sharp gaze to her short light summer dress down to her small bare feet. "What? Do you think I should change?" Her voice is husky and sweet.

I swallow as I direct my attention back on her face. "I think you're perfect." I hold out my hand. "Can I hope for a bikini under that thin dress?"

Cautiously, Elsie moves out of the kitchen. "No," she answers as she walks toward the hallway.

"Where are you going?" I lean against the bar to wait for her. I don't want to crowd her.

As she walks back out of the bedroom, I note the sunglasses on her head and book in her hand. "Getting ready for the pool." She smiles as she walks toward the door. As her hand grabs the doorknob the hotel phone rings. I shake my head with a smile as I walk to the phone to answer it.

"Yes?" I answer. "Sir, you have a message from a Natalie Derrikson to call her as soon as humanly possible."

"Thank you." I hang up. Elsie takes a couple of tentative steps towards me.

"Is everything okay?" The look of worry etched on her face.

"Yes, I guess my phone is off and my sister is trying to get ahold of me." Elsie visibly relaxes.

"Want me to stay?" Her tone gives me no clues to if she wants to stay or if she would rather go enjoy some sunshine.

"No, Else, I can take my phone down with me and call her." It only takes a few steps to bring myself to stand in front of her. I stroke her face lightly before I dash out of the hallway to the bedroom for my phone and grab some towels from the bathroom on my way back to her. "Ready?"

She nods with a soft smile on her face.

"Do you want to bring your phone?" I ask as she opens the door for us to exit.

Without looking at me she moves past me to leave, "No. I already talked to Mariah today. I have no one else who would need to get ahold of me." She pushes the elevator button then looks at me. "I'm not great at keeping up with my online presence."

I tuck her hair behind her ear, "that is so rare to find."

The ding of the elevator pulls her attention away from me. I follow her inside as the doors close behind me. The silence is comfortable, but I wish I had something to talk to her about. Elsie saves the day by speaking first. "I used to have a fear of getting phone calls." Her gaze lifts from the doors in front of us to me.

"Are you trying to give me more insight to you?" I smile at her as she searches my face.

"I guess so. Really, I have no idea why I felt the need to tell you that." Her brow furrows as she turns her attention back to the doors.

The ding chimes again as we reach the ground floor. She reaches for my hand as the doors open, together we exit and make our way to the pool area. There aren't as many people in the pool area as I would have thought but it is around dinner time. "Where would you like to put our stuff?"

"In the shade, please. I didn't bring sunblock."

"Excuse me," a woman walks closer to us, "I'm sorry I over-heard you; would you like to use my sunblock?"

Elsie smiles at the tall brunette with a bottle of sunblock in her hand. "I would be grateful if I could use some."

"Oh my god! I know that voice anywhere! Do you play *Annex*?" Elsie gives a small smile and nods, "You're Cybira!" The woman hops a little up and down. "Can I introduce you to my boyfriend?"

Elsie smiles but it isn't as genuine. She glances at me as the woman rushes over to the side of the pool. I don't notice the man getting out of the pool to make his way to us. I am too busy watching Elsie for any sign of her anxiety.

"Isn't this just the best stroke of luck?" The woman's voice is full of excitement.

CHAPTER 44

$\mathcal{E}$LSIE

"I'm sorry for her. Sometimes she just can't control her enthusiasm." The man next to her puts one hand around her waist and holds his other out for me. His blond hair steadily drips water to his shoulder which then makes a wet path down his muscular chest. He looks like he could be related to my book model Roland. Tentatively I take his hand and shake it. "I'm Jace, and this is my girlfriend, Melissa."

"Pleasure to meet you both. I'm..."

"Cybira. Mel told me."

I take my hand back from him and take a small step back. "I'm sorry, but how do you know that?" I look at his girlfriend.

"I have a knack for remembering voices. It is a freak superpower I possess." She offers me her sunblock. "I have been listening to the clan chat for months, but I am not sure of how to play well enough to do more than just a few easy assignments that Jace does with me when he isn't doing a takedown."

I smile at her as I take the bottle. "You can do some runs with me if you want to learn more." I reach for Bradley's hand and am relieved when he squeezes my hand in response. Vaguely I remember Bradley telling me he goes by Derrik when it isn't someone close to him. I take this opportunity to try that name on my tongue. "This is my fiancé, Derrik." He doesn't offer either of them a handshake. I watch Jace's gaze flow from my face, down my body, and back up to my eyes. Silently I thank myself for not taking off the sundress as soon as we entered the pool area. Suddenly swimming sounds like a bad idea. I don't know why my gut is giving off warning signs but so far in my life my gut has only been wrong once, and that had been alcohol induced. Almost on instinct I draw closer to Bradley.

Melissa looks from me, to Jace, then to Bradley. The smile she gives Bradley is perfect, enticing. "Do you play *Annex* too?" Melissa purrs.

"What's that?" Bradley looks down at me. "Is that the name of the game you like to play?"

I try to play off his lie. "The game I keep trying to get you to play? Yes."

"If you ever want to play and he doesn't, I'll play with you." Jace smiles but it is more of a leer.

"Jace..." Melissa's smile and flirting vanishes as she looks at Jace. Her brow furrows as she studies her boyfriend, his eyes still on me.

"We are going to the con on Friday. Maybe we will see you around." He smiles again before he heads toward the exit, Melissa in tow.

I can't help the shiver. Bradley releases my hand and puts his arm around me. He steers us to the other side of the pool to some seats. As I take a seat on the lounger, I see Bradley move to meet a member of the hotel staff. Our food is carried by a small woman who looks to be in her forties. Her dark hair is perfectly placed in a ponytail. She places the food on the table next to the lounger I am occupying. "Do you need anything else?" Her smile is warm.

"Thank you, I have everything I need." Bradley hands her cash before he turns to place the drinks on the table with our food.

"Would you like me to put some sunscreen on your back?" His voice is husky.

I can't help the incredulous look on my face. "Are you so impatient to put your hands on me?"

He leans down to kiss my cheek, his voice low in my ear, "you have no idea." As he stands back up, he makes quick work of opening the containers of food. His phone starts to ring as he moves to sit next to me. "Yea?" He answers like I do with Mariah.

I tune him out as I open my book, effectively giving him privacy and stepping back into the world I created as I read my newest installment of *Death Burns Within*.

CHAPTER 45

BRADLEY

"Do you have a few minutes?" Natalie's voice is a little distorted. "Sorry, I'm driving."

I glance over to Elsie, her food untouched, sunblock sitting next to her, her concentration solely for the book in her hand.

"Yea, I have a couple of minutes. I am sitting by the pool with Elsie." I grab my sandwich to take a bite.

"Oh? Am I interrupting?" I smile at her question.

"No. She's engrossed in a book right now." I tilt my head to see what she is so enthralled with. My heart sinks a little as I read the spine. *Shred the Shadow Book Six: Death Burns Within.* "Actually, give me a minute, okay?"

"Sure. Call me back in a bit." She hangs up before I put my phone down.

"Else?" I reach out to place my hand on her arm. She turns her head toward me but keeps her eyes on her book. She finally turns her clear grey eyes to me.

"Yes?" She looks around before looking back at me. "Everything okay?"

I grab the bottle next to her leg. "Before you get too far in your book would you like some sunscreen?" I jerk my head toward the table. "Or maybe you could eat something?"

Elsie bites her bottom lip as she looks at the table and then at the bottle in my hand. She nods once. She is graceful as she places the book in front of her, keeping her place in the book in the process. She gives me a shy smile as she crosses her arms in front of her to grab the bottom of the sundress she has on. My heart stutters as she raises her arms to pull the dress over her head. Her hair cascades down as she finishes taking the dress off. Her skin is pale but the light blue one piece makes her glow. Her hair falls in soft shiny dark waves to her waist.

"Everything okay?" Her voice is husky, but I can hear the worry in her quiet tone.

I try not to audibly gulp. "Yea. Do you need help with this?" I hold out the sunblock. She smiles and shakes her head as she takes it. I should look away as she applies it to her arms, legs, chest, and face, but I don't. I'm not the only one to take notice of Elsie.

"Hot tub was nice, but the view out here is so much better." A newly familiar voice has Elsie freezing while rubbing the white lotion on her arm. "Would you like to get into the water?"

She shields her eyes as she looks up at the man stopped in front of her lounger. "I can't swim, and I really want to read my book and enjoy my time with my fiancé."

"I'll hold on to you, baby." Jace's voice is smooth.

I don't move to look at Jace; it is taking all I have to not beat the hell out of the man, but I'm not willing to go to jail for this slimeball. I'm also afraid of scaring Elsie or overstepping myself. Too many things running through my head at once.

"What part of 'I have a fiancé' do you not understand?" Her tone is sharp, and her stare is hard.

"Nothing set in stone. I can show you some fun." He tries to entice her with a smile.

Elsie's gaze cuts to mine, panic close to the surface. Before I can move to put this asshole in his place Jace makes a move. He leans down, grabs Elsie by the back of the head and tries to pull her face to his. I land a punch to his face as Elsie's knee connects with his manhood. Jace falls sideways. His fingers still in Elsie's hair as he rolls to the ground. Elsie fights to disengage Jace from his hold on her hair.

"Let her go, now." My tone sounds as deadly as I feel. Jace groans and releases her. "Don't ever, and I mean ever, touch her or come near her again. You will regret your life if you think about not heeding my words."

"Sir, I am going to need you to come with me." A member of the hotel staff bends to help Jace up. It takes a few minutes and another man to help get Jace up and out of the pool area.

Elsie takes a deep breath. "Sorry" she whispers.

"Why are you sorry?" I hold out my arms for her, hoping she takes the offered hug.

"I should have handled that better." She moves into my arms, her own arms coming around my middle. Elsie tucks her head under my chin. I kiss the top of her head.

"You did nothing wrong. I am sorry it took me so long to get myself under control. I really wanted to beat the life out of him."

Her giggle is soft and shakes her body against mine, "I'm glad you didn't resort to violence until I did. I prefer you without a criminal history."

"I feel like we have been together so long that everything I do is just second nature." I try to keep my voice even despite the emotion I feel in my heart and the rush of adrenaline I just had in dealing with Jace. "Does that make sense?"

Elsie pulls away enough to look at me, her arms still around me. "Yes." She whispers, "I feel like I am whole. I don't have to worry about what is to come when it comes to you."

I give her a light kiss at the same time my phone starts to ring again. Elsie giggles against my lips. I can't help the groan as I pull away to answer it. "You ruined a moment." I feel Elsie disengage from me. My eyes follow her as I watch her walk to the steps into the pool. "Sorry to interrupt. I need to talk to you. Much easier now that I am not driving." My sister sounds annoyed.

"Okay, I am all ears; what do you need to talk about?" I lean back on the lounger and watch as Elsie goes underwater and comes back up. My gaze scans the rest of the area for any threats, but I am happy to see there is only one other couple left. Both seem to be in their mid-forties, lounging, while holding hands. I feel hope slice through me as I look from them to Elsie, maybe one day that will be us.

My sister's voice recaptures my attention. "Seth got wind that *Death Burns Within* got an HBO mini-series offer. Also, Showtime and Cinemax gave offers to buy the rights as well." Natalie's tone is apprehensive. "So, he thinks we should submit the lawsuit for the copyright infringement before anyone signs off on a TV show."

My gaze flicks to the book laying on the lounger by my feet. "Have you read any of the books?" I can't help but wonder if we are jumping the gun on suing. My brother put his best friend in charge of maintaining *Annex*'s brand and image before *Annex* was the empire it is today.

"I don't read fantasy." Natalie admits. "But if Seth thinks we should do something and maybe we should listen to him. I mean we do pay him to manage a department that their sole purpose is to look out for our brand." She sighs. "But I don't know firsthand if this suit has merit."

"You're right, we do pay him to keep track of this kind of thing." I grab my soda from the table next to me. "What else did you need to talk about?" I suck down half the soda before putting it back on the table.

I hear Natalie take a deep breath. "There is a ton of negative comments coming out against Elsie, in response to you both being engaged." I hear typing on Natalie's end. "I have been doing some digging. These mostly seem to be coming from people that know the woman helping at the Q and A."

"Mariah." I pinch the bridge of my nose as I close my eyes. "What is being said?"

"Do you really want to know?"

"I don't like to be blindsided," I answer.

"Fair enough." More clicking comes from Natalie's end. "She is being called a gold digger, a slut, and one particularly angry male is saying he has firsthand knowledge of how big of a whore she is."

"Do you believe any of them?" I keep my tone down.

Without hesitation she replies, "No."

"What is the name of the guy calling her a whore?" I try to keep my temper in check, I watch Elsie wade in the pool, not daring to go too deep.

Natalie is quiet for a moment. "I will find out; I didn't think to note it. You do have a plan, don't you?"

I can't help the smile that comes. "Of course, have you ever known me not to?"

"I remember growing up you were quick to react and land in a ton of trouble."

"I've grown up a little since then," I argue.

"Do you need any help with your plans?"

"Let me see what you find out and see if I can get any information from Elsie. I am going to go spend more time with Else. I will text you later." I hang up before I hear her reply. As I stand to take off my shirt so I can join Elsie in the pool, I note that she hasn't eaten anything.

CHAPTER 46

ELSIE

I can't help my laughter as I watch Bradley run and cannonball into the deep end of the pool. I'm still laughing as he swims under the water toward me. He smiles as he surfaces in front of me. "Well, fancy meeting you here." His tone is playful. I feel his hand on my waist. "Do you really not know how to swim?"

"I know how to swim; I just don't like if my feet can't touch the bottom." I feel heat on my face. I look around and see we are alone in the pool. "Or swimming with strangers."

"What if I hold on to you and carry you into the deep end?"

I try to think of something else to avert the fear comes with thinking of being in deep water. I don't notice the tears rolling down my face. I have no idea how long we stand waist deep in the water, but as soon as I feel his arms come around me, I feel myself relax instantly.

"What's wrong, Else?" Bradley strokes my hair as he plants a kiss on my forehead. It takes real effort to pull myself out of the darkness in my mind. I force my eyes to open to look into Bradley's. His lips are warm on my cheek as he tries to comfort me. "You can trust me. I would never let anything happen to you."

I use all my brain power to shove the bad thoughts down. When I finally feel in control again, I give Bradley a small smile. "Could we stay in the shallow end for a little bit? I don't typically get into water."

His nod eases my anxiety. "Do you know how to float?"

A deep feeling of pure trepidation settles in my stomach. I shake my head to avoid my voice giving away the depth of my fear.

"Put your legs up into my arms," Bradley instructs as I feel his arm settle across my shoulders.

"Do you swear on everything you hold dear not to let me go?" I stop myself from asking him to pinkie promise me.

"I swear on everything I love; I will not let you go. I will keep you in the shallow side." His smile is encouraging, "have a little trust in me."

In no time he has me floating on my own. This man is so patient with me. I'm not sure what I ever did to deserve him, but I am so grateful for finding him.

Dinner poolside was perfect. Once we got out, I discovered swimming makes a girl famished. After we finished dinner, we went back upstairs to our room. I went straight to the shower when I got in the door. The smile hasn't left my face even as I finish washing my hair. I hear the bathroom door open; I can see Bradley through the frosted glass. "I was just seeing if you needed me to set your clothes in here."

"You know, if you got in here with me, we could save some water..." I can't help the giggle that escapes as I watch a grown man move so quickly to remove his clothes.

"I could get used to taking my shower with you every day." His voice is thick as his hands claim my waist.

"Can you now?" I try to sound serious.

"I was serious when I told you I would book us tickets to Vegas, Else." His gaze is intense. I feel the sincerity in his tone. If I am being honest with myself, I would probably follow him down that aisle and never feel one shred of apprehension or fear doing so. "What are you thinking?"

"That a part of me agrees, Vegas would be great." I busy myself with rinsing my hair to avoid looking at him.

I feel his hands move from my waist to my wrists. "Else, I'm serious. I'd marry you in a second."

I open my eyes to look into his, "I know." I whisper. "A part of me really wants to, but the more rational side of my brain thinks we should take things slow. Actually, learn about each other."

"We have known each other for—"

"But knowing someone online is not the same as knowing them in real life," I interrupt him.

"Have I proven I was someone different in game?"

I hesitate to answer him. "No. But it also has only been a matter of days. I don't feel wanting more time before making that kind of commitment is asking a lot."

He pulls me to him as he lowers his head to kiss me. My entire body reacts to him. There is no doubt that the chemistry is there, I just don't want to have any regrets by rushing into things. If I had to live in this moment for the rest of my life, I would be sufficiently happy. But all good things must come to an end, and my life is no exception to that.

CHAPTER 47

BRADLEY

We finish our shower and get dressed in comfortable silence. I hope she is thinking about what I said. I watch as she moves around the penthouse. "Else, what are you doing?"

"I'm thinking. I have to keep busy when I am brainstorming," she answers as I watch her collect our used towels from the bathroom.

"Do you ever just sit and relax?" Elsie tenses at my question.

She stops to look at me. "Does it bother you if I am constantly in motion?"

I think about that for a second. "No, but I feel guilty not doing something to help."

She smiles at me. "If I need help, I will ask for it. No need to feel guilty." She tilts her head. "Would you help me?"

I toss the remote onto the coffee table as I stand. "Sure, what do you need, Else?" It only takes me three steps to make my way to her.

"Is that your normal response when someone asks you for help?"

"You're welcome to call and ask my sister if my responses are true to my real character." I reach into my pocket to hand her my phone.

She looks down at the device. "Why are you handing me that?"

"You are welcome to use my phone or look in it anytime you feel like it. Call my family. Do anything you need, so you have the reassurance." I smile at her. "My passcode is 8891."

She looks up at me, tears in her eyes. "Mine is 9813." The tears spill one at a time down her face as she softly cries. "There is something I need to talk to you about."

"You can tell me anything, Else." I reach out to wipe the tears off her face.

Before she can utter one syllable Elsie's phone rings. "Sorry, hold that thought." She smiles as she holds up her finger before answering the phone. She hits speaker phone then places the phone on top of the back of the couch. Elsie goes back to cleaning up the penthouse. "Hiya?" Her tone is light.

"Um, we have a bit of a problem at home." Mariah sounds apprehensive.

Elsie sighs as she glances at her phone. "Daniel?"

"Yes, how did you..." Mariah pauses mid-sentence before yelling, "He called you didn't he?" Mariah sounds horrified.

Elsie shrugs even though Mariah cannot see her. "Yea, he didn't mince words."

"Oh, Elizabeth, I am so sorry. The nerve of that man."

"He's your brother. Don't be too hard on him." Elsie leans against the back of the couch, her phone resting next to her arm.

Mariah audibly huffs. "Guess I can't choose my blood relations."

Elsie smiles toward her phone. She pulls a lock of hair over her shoulder and begins playing with it. "So, what is the problem?"

Mariah doesn't speak for a long moment. "I am worried about you being in the wedding."

Elsie stops playing with her hair instantly. She closes her eyes and takes a deep breath. "I will do anything you want; it is your wedding."

"Daniel is bringing Colin as his plus one. I just don't want you to be put in a bad situation." Mariah's voice is soft.

"I'll be with her, there isn't anything to worry about." I offer Elsie a smile, her eyes search my face before she lets out a dejected noise.

"Don't worry about me. I'm sure we can celebrate properly after you are back from your honeymoon."

Mariah lets out a frustrated scream. "Why does it feel like this is one of the biggest days of my life, but I really have no control over any of it?"

"Mariah, if you want me there, I will make it happen. I am not the bride, that choice is totally up to you."

Another moment of silence. "If you guys want to just come as guests for now until I figure out my life, that would be easier on me," Mariah finally confesses.

"Absolutely. Really, Mariah, don't worry about me." Elsie is back to playing with her hair. "I always just want you to be happy."

Listening and watching the exchange between the two women is awkward and heartbreaking. Mariah finally ends the call promising to call Elsie back later.

"Come here, Else." I wrap my arms around her. An idea forming, but I need to hammer it out before I go to Elsie with it. I feel her body shudder and her arms tighten around me. I hear her quiet sobs. It feels like second nature to tighten my arms around her, my hands smoothing her long hair to comfort her. "Everything is going to be fine. I promise."

I hold Elsie until her tears run out. She moves to disengage from me. "Thank you. I don't normally get that upset or cry. But for some reason today was the culmination of proof I belong nowhere."

My heart breaks listening to her. "What if we still show up to support her anyway?"

Her brows knit together for a moment as she thinks. The color drains from her face. "I don't ever want you to meet Mariah's brothers." She wraps herself close to me, her whisper barely audible. "It would kill me if they turned you against me too."

"Honey, no one could ever turn me against you." I kiss the top of her head. "Come on, let's have a snack picnic in the living room and watch whatever makes you happy."

I pull her with me as I move to seat her on the couch. "Now, you sit right here, and I will be right back." I give her a quick peck on the lips before I go to the kitchen for some snacks.

"If you could give me a moment." Elsie's tone is fraught with emotions, that she is trying hard to contain. I expect her to flee from the room and fling herself onto her bed, to bury her face in her pillow while she sobs. Natalie has forced me to watch plenty of those fairytale movies when she was younger. The minutes tick by as I give Elsie her moment. She opens her mouth to say something but instead shakes her head. "Sometimes, I am forced to remember that I can't find the best out of every situation."

"Do you want to talk about it?" I wish I could just look into her head to see exactly what she is thinking.

"Why?" Her brows knit together for a moment, "you heard everything. Why dwell on it?"

"Talking might help."

"'Help' what?" She shrugs her shoulders. "She might be my chosen family but that doesn't mean that I trump her actual family." Elsie gives me a sad smile. "Mariah is always trying to please her brothers. Their opinion of her carries more weight with her. I know that."

"You are worth being put first!" It takes restraint to keep my tone at a conversation level. I am not mad at her, I am angry that there are people in the world who would make this beautiful, smart, and amazing woman think she is worthless.

Elsie turns her clear light grey eyes on me. I hold her gaze, the magnitude of what I just said heavy in the air. She searches my face.

"Why do you have to say things like that?" she whispers.

"Because I feel that you undervalue yourself. I don't know where that comes from but I feel compelled to reiterate that you are worthy of love, attention, and consideration,"

I don't get to finish as I feel the warmth of her body on mine. Her arms squeeze around me tight as she buries her face in my chest. It feels more and more like second nature, her embracing me. I pull her closer to me. We stand there like that for what seems like hours, in actuality it is only a few minutes.

The phone rings in the penthouse once again interrupting our moment. I feel the loss of heat as Elsie disengages to release me. "Hello?" It takes effort to not sound annoyed.

"Hey, can I talk to Elsie?" Natalie sounds excited.

"Let me ask her if she wants to talk to you, this is the second time you have interrupted us," I chide.

CHAPTER 48

$\mathcal{E}$LSIE

"Else, my sister would like to talk to you. Feel free to say, no." His smile is infectious.

I hold out my hand for the phone, a smile taking over. Before he hands it to me, he hits a button and places the receiver on the table. Bradley's hands are in my hair, his body pushing mine back until my back is against the wall. He is a man possessed. His lips move against mine. It is as if he had not seen me in ages. I mimic his actions, his passion. I follow his lead. Finally, Bradley slowly lets up. His fingers are still tangled in my hair, his body still pressed against mine.

I brush my nose against his. "Hm what was that for?"

"I was taking back the moment she interrupted."

"You have me thinking about Vegas," I whisper. For a fraction of a second, I worry I have ruined the mood.

"I'll call the airport now, honey." He moves to kiss my neck.

I step away from him. "Give me the phone, you are such a mean brother." I grab the phone off the table and hit the button to take her off hold. "Hello?"

"I'm sorry I ruined your moment." Natalie's voice sounds remorseful.

I turn and shake my head at Bradley. He grins as he leans against the wall to wait for me to get done with the call. "Don't worry, you can interrupt anytime." Natalie giggles, Bradley on the other hand raises a heavy brow as his grin vanishes. "If your brother plays his cards right, he might have many more moments."

Without saying a word, he steps closer to me and takes my hands in his. Bradley kisses the top of my hands before placing them on his heart. No words need spoken.

"What can I do for you?" I ask Natalie, my gaze never leaving Bradley's.

There is a brief pause. "I was wondering if maybe I could come get you and we could go out for a little while. I know you probably aren't going to be in town for long." She takes a breath.

"You are right about that. I actually have a con to go to on Friday, then Friday night I have to be on a plane to get back home for Mariah's wedding Saturday..." I trail off remembering I technically don't have to be there for the wedding. My heart hurts for a moment. I try to think of something else to avert my attention.

"So, do you have plans right now?" Natalie's voice is hopeful.

"I would love to hang out with you." I take a deep breath, "but would it be ok if you came here and hang out with me? I am not comfortable going out in such a big city."

"I think the hotel has a bar we can grab a drink at and then head back up to the room if you still want to hang out." She sounds hesitant. I have to remember she is younger and likes the bar scene. This is a compromise for both of us.

"All right, one drink and then we are coming back up to the room, deal?"

"Deal!" Natalie lets out a small squeal. "I have to be dreaming." She takes a deep breath. "Okay, I will be there in about a half hour or so."

"Okay, see you in a bit." I hang up the phone.

"So, you are going to hang out with my sister?" Bradley tucks my hair behind my ear.

"How long does it take you to lose interest in a woman?" My question renders him speechless for a moment.

He tilts his head. "What makes you think I would lose interest in you?" Sadness and concern cross his face.

"I'm trying to figure out why me."

He gives me a soft smile as he leans his forehead to mine. "I am terrified I'm going to wake up and you will be a figment of my imagination."

I can't help but roll my eyes at the cliché statement.

"You know there is a reason that saying is a cliché." He pulls me in close. "Doesn't change the fact that it's true."

I shake my head softly as I pull away from him. "I am going to change so I look decent for your sister."

"Why?"

"Because I want to make a good impression on her."

"She already thinks you are amazing. She might be your second biggest fan." A wide sexy smile spreads across his face.

"Second?"

"No one can top how much I admire you." He shrugs his shoulder.

I roll my eyes as I turn to walk into the bedroom. A thought crosses my mind as I open the closet door and stare at the dresses I have hanging. "Um, Bradley?"

I am amused that I don't jump or feel anything except comfort as his arms circle my waist from behind. "Yes, my love?"

"Would you go down to the bar with me?" I lean my head back to rest on his shoulder.

"Afraid of being alone with my sister?" he jokes.

"Bars make me nervous." I mentally curse myself for not having a spare pair of jeans. "I need to go back to the house I rented so I can get my stuff for tomorrow." Bradley releases me so I can move again. I grab a dress from the small closet and my Raven bag. "I'm going to get ready." He kisses my cheek before I leave the bedroom and close the door to the bathroom.

CHAPTER 49

*B*RADLEY

My phone rings as I enter the kitchen. "Hello?"

"Hey, I got your number from Mariah. My groomsmen are coming out here to have my bachelor party tonight! I wanted to know if you would like to join us." Nate's voice is the most jovial I have ever heard him.

"What time and where?" I ask.

"Mariah said you are staying at the Hilton; they have a nice bar, right?" Nate takes a second, his voice lowers. "I was banned from having a stripper or going to a club." He sighs. "My groomsmen want to find a club, but I really don't want to go against Mariah. I know how I would feel if I had told her not to do something and she ignored me."

My opinion on Nate goes up a few points. Good man. "Give me a minute to make sure I don't have anything going on." I push the mute button; Elsie's voice gets a little louder the closer I get to the bathroom. "Hey, Else?" I knock on the bathroom door.

"Come in." The music stops as I open the door. She turns to look at me, I swear my heart stops for a moment. Her makeup is lightly done, and her hair has big curls through it. The sundress she has picked out is a seafoam green. "Everything okay?" Her fingers touch my cheek bringing my gaze back to her own. The genuine concern in her eyes is proof that she cares for me.

"Nate got my number and wants me to meet him for drinks with his groomsmen. I wanted to make sure we didn't have plans later on. I figured after you and Natalie come up to the room, I could head out with him for a bit."

Elsie's lips purse as she grabs a lock of her hair. "Yea, sure. We don't have plans." Elsie's eyes are full of emotions I can't begin to dissect.

Part of me really wants to give Nate an excuse but a bigger part of me wants to give my sister and Elsie time to bond. I reason with myself that I will be inside the hotel, so I won't be too far from her. I pull my phone back out and push the button to speak to Nate, "Yea, I will meet you at nine-thirty. Does that work for you?"

"Great! See you in a bit!" He hangs up before I do.

I slide my phone into my back pocket. "Come here." I reach out for Elsie. "What's wrong, honey?"

She buries her head in my chest. With little effort I lift her to sit her on the counter of the bathroom, she moves her head from my chest to my neck.

"Do you want to talk about why you are upset that I am going out?" I keep my tone soft.

"I'm not upset you are going out." She inhales before I feel her lips touch my neck. "I'm sad that what we have is ending." Her voice breaks.

A deep-set panic sets in as her words register in my brain. "Why is it ending?"

She moves her head so she can look at me. Tears slowly roll down her cheeks. Her eyes close as she bows her head, a clear sign of defeat. She shakes her head. "Nate's groomsmen are Mariah's brothers."

"Do you trust me?" Her skin is soft under my fingers as I lift her chin to look at me. "Let's just pretend they are The Council. We can run this takedown with our eyes closed." I kiss her lips, pouring as much confidence and reassurance into it as I can. With a little patience I get her to respond to my kiss.

"I'm not ready to lose you," she whispers as she breaks our contact.

"Wait here." I leave the room only to retrieve the small box out of our bedroom. "I was going to wait for a more grandiose moment, but this feels like the right moment." I grab Elsie's hand and gently tug her off the counter, as she stands, I drop to one knee, with the small box opened. Everything in my life feels like it is lining up perfectly leading up to this one moment in time. "Elizabeth, I found you by chance and have conquered the world in *Annex*. I want this to be the beginning of our forever, the beginning of our ultimate takedown, to face this world together, for the rest of our lives. Will you marry me?"

CHAPTER 50

ELSIE

He nailed my perfect proposal, the one thing I never thought I would need or want to hear. The one thing I have found to be exactly what I need. He is so patient kneeling before me in this hotel bathroom. Absolute perfection. He understands me without much effort. I don't think I could write a more perfect partner for anyone.

I end his suspense. "Yes, I'll marry you." He takes the ring out of the box and places it on my finger. He kisses my hand before his lips devour mine. This kiss is full of more than passion. Minutes pass, he is hesitant to release me. I keep my hands on his face. "After you spend time with Nate and the other guys, I will not hold you to this engagement."

"That hurts, baby." His voice is the same low baritone that soothes my nerves.

"I need you to know that." I run my fingers through his hair. "I would never want—" His fingers thread through my hair, he gently tugs my hair, so my head tilts up.

"I know you better than any of them." He interrupts. "I also swear I will never expose you or Mariah's secrets."

I can't help the tears that follow as I smile at him. "Thank you for understanding me."

"Now, let's get ready to hang out with my sister!" He winks. "And show her your ring."

"You want to tell her?"

"Of course. She is going to be ecstatic." He kisses my nose as he leaves me in the bathroom.

I glance at my reflection. It only takes a moment to fix the light makeup I have applied. I hear the phone in the room ring. I walk out just as Bradley hangs up.

"Natalie is downstairs. I told her we would be down in a second." Bradley's gaze rakes down my body and back up. "You are so beautiful, honey."

I can't help the blush that creeps up my face. "Thank you."

"Are you going to take a purse or your phone?" he asks as I walk to the door to leave.

I shake my head, "I don't need my purse." I shrug. "And who needs a phone when you are spending time with people? I'm not leaving the hotel, so it really isn't necessary."

"Well, okay then. Let's go." His hand rests on my hip as we walk to the elevator.

"I need you to know," I look up at the man who has come to mean more to me than any other man, ever in my life, "I love you."

His grip on me tightens for a moment, a thrill shoots through me. "I love you, too." He kisses the top of my head. "I think I have loved you since the second you spoke at that first takedown."

I elbow him in the side. "Be serious." I roll my eyes.

He looks down at me, his gaze mesmerizing, "I'm one hundred percent serious, I tried to tell myself I was just interested in you. I lied to myself. I would be sad if you weren't online to talk to, or if you logged off before me, my world got a little darker." He sighed, "when I decided to find out more about you, I was looking for a flaw, a reason to not look for you." He shakes his head, "then my crazy sister got in on it and wouldn't stop talking about why she loved your books and listening to you at your events." He gives me a bright smile, "I was sunk from the very beginning."

"I might have been too." I admit, "your voice has always been a comfort to me. You made takedowns easier just by being in my groups. It didn't matter what you were saying, your voice felt like home."

The elevator door opens and all I hear is a restrained scream. "Elsie!" I look around for the source of the sound. Natalie is excitedly jumping up and down waving her arm in the air. "Over here."

"I'm here." I can't help but laugh.

"Have a little bit of restraint." Bradley looks so serious while quietly speaking to her. I love that she rolls her eyes at his stuffiness.

"Let's go get a drink." She links her arm with mine and pulls me towards the bar.

"I got it, what do you both want?" Bradley offers.

"I want a hurricane." Natalie doesn't look at him when she answers. I look up at him. "I have no idea. I don't drink alcohol normally."

"How about I get you a virgin hurricane?" I am grateful that he keeps his voice low so only I can hear.

"Please." I give him a quick kiss before he walks to the bar.

"Let's sit over there," Natalie says as she pulls me over to a booth against the wall. As we sit, I see Bradley make his way to us expertly holding three drinks.

I can't help but feel like Natalie and I are kindred. Not just because we both love Bradley, differently but deeply. Her energy just jives well with my own.

"I am trying so hard not to fangirl right now," Natalie admits before she takes a long pull from her straw.

I feel Bradley's arm settle on my waist, once more. "You are covering it very well," I reassure her. I reach out to position my straw so I can take a drink.

Natalie grabs my hand to pull my ring closer to inspect. Her gaze is sharp as she looks from the ring to Bradley. "That is a beautiful ring, Elsie." She releases me.

"Thank you." I look between the siblings; they seem to be in a stare down. "I'm going to use the restroom." Bradley moves to let me out of the booth. He kisses my cheek before I head toward the sign for the bathroom.

CHAPTER 51

BRADLEY

"You're serious about her, aren't you?" My sister's tone is mostly disbelief.

"Spending the last few days with her just solidified that she is exactly who she portrayed herself to be. I couldn't imagine anyone being more perfect for me." My sister brushes a tear from her eye.

"Did you propose properly?" She gives me a stern look.

I take a drink from my beer. "I think I did?" My tone is more of a question than assurance.

Natalie shakes her head, but her smile is wide. "I am just so happy; it is like a dream come true." Her restraint is obvious as she talks about Elsie. Her smile vanishes just as quickly as it had appeared, "Have you talked to Shane to tell him about your news?"

My hand rubs the back of my neck. "He isn't interested in my personal life, Nat. You know he is elbow deep in that new expansion we are launching in seven months."

"It wouldn't hurt you to call him." She looks just like Mom with her hand on her hip, even sitting down she is feisty. "Mom would love her."

I leave the statement hanging in the air between us. Things

between our parents and us are strained at best. None of us like to discuss the latest argument with them.

Natalie tips her head to the side as she studies me.

"What are you looking at me like that for?" I polish off my beer.

"I wonder what Elsie would say about our parents." She shakes her head as she gives an anxious little laugh before taking another drink of her beverage.

The crowd parts slightly as Elsie makes her way back to us. Her face is paler than usual. Her eyes keep darting back and forth eyeing the people she passes with trepidation. Natalie notices too. She follows me out of the booth to meet Elsie. "Hey, Else?" I reach out to hold on to her as she struggles to gather her calm. "Do you want to go back up to the room?"

Elsie closes her eyes for a moment. "Yes, please," she softly begs. I watch her reach out and grab Natalie's hand. The three of us move to the elevators. Elsie doesn't start to relax until we are back in the room.

"Could I have a minute, please?" She grabs her phone and turns to walk into our bedroom. She closes the door behind her.

"I should have remembered she isn't a fan of crowds," Natalie whispers.

I pat her on the back before I turn towards the kitchen to make Elsie a glass of ice water. I hear the bathroom door close and notice my sister isn't in the living room anymore. Assuming she is in the bathroom I take a seat on the couch to wait for one or both to come out to join me. I hear my sister come out of the bathroom; she makes a bee line for me.

"She's on the phone with someone," Natalie whispers.

"So?" I can't help the incredulous smile.

"Something happened down in the bar," Natalie hisses, frustrated with me.

I hurry to the bathroom to listen through the closed door to our bedroom. Natalie is right beside me listening too.

"Elizabeth I swear I didn't know he invited anyone other than my brothers to come out for his bachelor party." Mariah is on speaker; she is the only one speaking. "Please say something."

I hear muffled crying. I give my sister a warning glance. She steps away from me as I force the door open. Elsie is laying on the bed, her face in my pillow, sobs shake her body. "Elsie!" Mariah yells not knowing what happened. "Are you ok?" Panic laces her tone.

"Elsie will have to call you back." I keep my tone low as I end the call. With minimal effort I pull her up in my arms to cradle her against my chest. I rock her softly as she cries into my neck. Elsie places her free hand over my heart. I smooth her hair while I wait for her to cry all her sadness out.

"Else?" I finally feel like I can speak. "Do you need something?"

She shakes her head against my neck. Her sobs slow, her body finally stops shaking. "I'm sorry," she whispers, her breath hot against my skin, her head still on my shoulder.

"You did nothing wrong, honey." I tighten my hold on her. "Do you want to tell me what happened?"

She is silent for a few minutes. Finally, she speaks, her tone the softest whisper. "Nate and Mariah's brothers are here. I knew that, but Daniel also brought Colin with him. When I went to the bathroom, he was outside the door waiting for me." She takes a deep breath.

"Did he touch you?" I try to keep my anger in check.

Again, she shakes her head. "No, he cornered me." Her hand over my heart moves to around my neck as she gets closer. "He said he was happy I decided to see reason and come to him." She hiccups. "That he will do me the favor of making me feel good again but only if I keep it a secret since I'm only good enough as a side piece." She moves to disengage from me. "I'm a loyal and pretty pet."

I don't let her move from my lap. "Elizabeth, look at me." She takes a moment to comply. "I need you to hear me. You are an amazing woman." I wipe a new tear from her cheek as it starts to roll. "You are interesting, funny, witty, and determined." She gives me a brittle smile. "You are generous, and I am so grateful that we found each other."

She gasps as I finish my small speech. "I'm terrified they are going to poison you against me." Her gaze drops.

"I have great faith in myself and in what we have." I move my head to kiss her. She reluctantly returns the kiss. "I love you, Else."

She traces my jawline with her nail, my skin prickles at the sensation. "I love you too, Bradley."

"Let's get back out there with my sister." Elsie nods as she stands, together we walk out of the bedroom.

Natalie is changing channels on the tv lounging on the couch like she does it all the time. She silently watches us enter the living room and sit on the couch opposite her.

"So, who do I need to kill?" She finally speaks.

To my relief Elsie giggles. I feel my body relax at the sound. "No one." She grabs a lock of hair to play with. "I prefer if my sister-in-law not do hard time."

Natalie visibly holds in her excitement before she speaks again. "How about we order some Chinese and watch some bad TV and we can just hang out? I always wanted a sister growing up, but I got saddled with two blockhead brothers."

Elsie nods as a big smile lights up her face, "What is your other brother like?"

"He looks just like Bradley; except he has blond hair," Natalie answers. "He is a big computer buff, so he rarely looks up from a screen to bother talking to anyone." My sister rolls her eyes.

CHAPTER 52

*E*LSIE

I adore how Natalie is trying so hard to forget who I am while she talks to me. Her tone keeps slipping a few octaves as she speaks. It is endearing. "Chinese and bad TV sound perfect."

Natalie lets out a small shriek as she pulls out her phone. "What would you like to eat?"

"Shrimp fried rice and two eggrolls." I turn to Bradley who grabs hold of my hand. "Are you hungry?"

"Order me a General Tso's chicken and a few eggrolls. I will eat them when I get back up here."

"Where are you going?" Natalie looks up from her phone for a moment as she asks.

"Nate invited me out for his bachelor party, and I would like to get to know him better." Bradley sounds genuine. I just hope this isn't the end of us and I won't have to reinvent myself again.

"Bradley, could you toss a text to Mariah that I am okay but that I want to be left alone right now? I'm sure she is blowing up my phone."

"Of course, Else." The couch moves a little as he shifts to get his phone out of his back pocket to send the text. I hear his phone go off almost as soon as he hits send.

"Hello?" He keeps his voice level. His gaze shifts to me. "She is hanging out with my sister tonight." He glances at Natalie before pinching the bridge of his nose. "I know you are, but you need to accept that right this moment she is exactly where she wants to be with the people she wants to be around." He shakes his head as he opens his eyes, "I promise I will take the best care of her."

He puts his phone down as he hangs up. "No goodbye?" I can't help the smile that accompanies the question.

He shakes his head, a small smile appearing on his own face. "Do I look okay to go socialize with the boys?" He gestures at his clothes.

I run a critical assessment over him. "As long as you are comfortable." I don't need to tell him he looks sexy; he knows.

He gives me a challenging stare. I roll my eyes at his obvious antics to get me to admit he is hot. "You know you aren't ugly!" The exasperation in Natalie's voice unmistakable.

Bradley turns his head with a bright smile. "I know, I just wanted to hear her say it." His gaze cuts to me. "Well? How do I look?"

I look from Bradley to Natalie. "Our numbers don't match, do they?" I pose the question to Natalie. Since she is such a fan of my books she understands my question right away.

Natalie looks at her brother and then back to me,."I think I am not qualified to answer that just like you aren't objective enough to answer it either." Natalie puts her phone down next to her. "My brother has a very low number on that scale because he is my brother. You are beautiful, Elsie, even if you aren't aware of it. You are a solid eight and a half." She tilts her head toward her brother as she assesses him. "But my brother a five at best." She shrugs.

"Are you ranking my looks?" Bradley feigns being affronted.

"It is a system Elsie writes about in her stories." Natalie giggles. "You are overly critical of yourself, Elsie."

"Probably." I try to pull my melancholy mood back up. Running into Colin earlier threw me off.

"Honey?" Bradley nudges my shoulder with his, "I'm going to go downstairs for a bit. I will be back in a little while." He kisses my cheek.

"I'm going downstairs to the lobby to grab the food." Natalie stands. "And to give you both a little privacy for a moment."

I see Bradley nod as Natalie makes her way to the door and out of the penthouse.

"Come here, honey." Bradley pulls me closer to him. I put my arms around his middle, my head on his chest positioned so I can hear his heartbeat. I hear him inhale as he pulls me close to him. "Else?"

"Hmmm?" I take comfort in him holding me.

"I won't go if you really don't want me to." His low baritone tickles my ear but makes the butterflies in my stomach take flight as I feel his fingers comb through my hair.

I can't help the sigh that escapes me, "No. You're right. I need to trust that our relationship is solid even against outside forces." I lift my face to kiss his jaw. "Just please, don't feed into their talk or reveal any of Mariah's secrets, or mine."

His arms tighten their hold on me. "I love you, Else."

"I love you too, Bradley."

We pull apart when we hear Natalie come back in the room. Bags in both of her hands. "Don't mind me, I will busy myself in the kitchen." She calls out before turning to get into the kitchen. "There was a couple of envelopes downstairs for you Elsie. I'll leave them on the counter for you."

"Be good while I'm gone." I get up with him to walk him to the door. "Have fun you two." He calls to his sister before giving me a quick kiss. "Text me if you need me, Else." The door closes behind him.

CHAPTER 53

BRADLEY

As I stroll into the bar for the second time in the same night, I notice Nate right away. He stands to wave me over. The three men at the pub table with him all stop talking to look at me as I approach. "Hey!" Nate holds out his hand. "This is Derrik." His tone suggests they have heard of me but now they can put a name with the face. He points to the man across the table from me. "That is Marcus, Mariah's oldest brother and this is Daniel, Mariah's second oldest brother." He takes a moment for the guys to murmur hellos to me. "I'm Colin, basically another of Mariah's brothers." Colin holds out his hand for me. I nod my head at him avoiding his handshake as I flag down the waitress.

"I'd like a Guinness, please." She smiles as she walks to the bar. Colin lowers his hand from me, but he keeps his gaze on me.

"Are you excited about Saturday?" Marcus has to raise his voice to be heard over the conversation around us.

Nate shrugs as he takes a long pull from his beer. "Not excited. I will be happy when it is finally done so Mariah will go back to being normal. All this planning and her work has her exhausted and emotional."

Daniel laughs. "She's probably pregnant."

Nate pales as the words register. He shakes his head. "Dude! Shut up."

"Enjoy her only being crazy about the wedding because after the wedding it is only a matter of time before she starts nagging you for kids and a bigger house." Colin chuckles as he watches his friend.

"I was trying to convince her to move out here. It is so much better than Ohio," Nate laments.

"So, are you married, Derrik?" Marcus turns his attention to me.

"Nope." I keep my answers short, so I don't reveal too much, and I keep the interaction light. I want to hang out with Nate and see if we could be friends. I think it would be a good thing to be his friend if his wife is Elsie's best friend.

Nate looks at me quizzically, he is interrupted as the waitress brings me my beer and brings another round for the others.

"So, tell us about yourself, Derrik," Colin presses. "What do you do for a living, where are you from?"

Carefully I guard my answers. "I work for an online game company here in California."

"That's pretty cool." Daniel's tone is patronizing. "Getting paid to play videogames all day." I watch him roll his eyes at his brother. They share a snigger.

"Yes, I mean it is pretty cool, but I don't get paid to play it."

"Oh, poor you." Marcus says with another chuckle with his brother. "So what company do you work for?" He tips back another swig.

"I work for *Annex*." I watch as the men around the table exchange looks.

Colin speaks up first, "Hey that's cool man. It's like we all are on the same team." He raises his long neck towards the other guys before downing the rest.

"Yea? How so?" I try to keep my tone light.

"We all own a production company. We have a meeting with *Annex* the morning before the wedding." Daniel's tone is more boastful. "Our deal has been publicized about and anticipated for months now. This week marks the beginning of greatness and…"

"Cold hard cash!" All four men cheer.

"Nate, you're a part of this production company?" I take a long drink as I wait for his answer.

Nate nods, his tone enthusiastic. "Yep. My brothers in law are amazing at what they do. They are going to make a killing on this deal." He claps Marcus on the back as he looks at him with admiration, "This deal is going to set them up on Easy Street."

"Is it now?" I take another drink as I look from one man to the next. "Well, I wish you all the best of luck." I raise my beer up to them. My brain is rapidly hatching a plan.

"I'm shocked you aren't asking to join our company." Daniel cocks an eyebrow at me.

I manage to shrug while polishing off my beer.

"Apparently Derrik is with Elizabeth," Nate announces to the others. Daniel puts his long neck down forcefully, Marcus tries to catch himself as the announcement has him choking on his drink, and Colin's gaze gets harder.

I would love nothing more than to punch both men. Nate is not paying attention to any of them, his face is pale as he looks behind my shoulder. I follow his gaze and turn in time to see Mariah coming in the front door. Her face is red; anger radiating off her.

"You!" She points to our table, we look at each other before looking back at her. Still no indication who she is talking to or mad at. "Who the fuck do you think you are?" She comes to stand next to me her finger pointing at her brother, Daniel. He is still in a state of shock mixed with a few beers to register what she is saying, he stays silent.

"And you! Why the hell are you even here?" She turns to yell at Colin next. He takes a sip of beer to avoid speaking and earning more wrath.

"This is my wedding!" she seethes. "This is my special day and all of you have managed to ruin everything!" She slams her hands down on the pub table.

"Honey..." Nate moves over to her trying hard to quiet her and calm her at once.

"Don't you dare try and calm me down." She backs away from him. "I hate how awful you all are." Tears brim her eyes; I hand her a napkin. She looks at me before she takes it. "Thank you." She takes care to dab her eyes. "Is Elizabeth upstairs?" she asks me.

I nod. Before she or I can say anything else Colin opens his mouth.

"Elizabeth left, she was in the bar earlier." He takes another sip of beer.

"I just don't get why, after all this time, you all hate her so much!" Mariah wipes her eyes again.

"That bitch is a gold digger. She stuck around long enough to get our parent's money. She is a stuck-up bitch." Daniel's voice is unrestrained as he spews his hatred for my Elsie. "And now she has her claws in this poor sap. No offense, but maybe you should hear some things about her from her family before you decide to keep seeing her. Bitch is cold, has no feeling invested in anyone, and only cares about what she is getting out of the people she put herself close to." He polishes off his beer. "She stuck around long enough until our parents got sick and never even once came back to check on them, bitch didn't even bother coming to their funeral." He shakes his head with a cruel smile. "She is a selfish human. I'm glad my parents never adopted her."

Marcus nods in agreement and adds, "No idea why she has agreed to be with you, can't hope for much from a wannabe pro gamer. Maybe she's just with you out of boredom." He gives me a once over before chuckling into his bottle as he takes another drink.

"She's a whore, man." Colin's voice is louder than it needs to be. "Must really be desperate to be with a woman like her. Do you have no standards? What kind of lies has she told you?"

I feel something on my chest, I look down and see Mariah's hand on me. She shakes her head. I have to consciously make myself unclench my fists. I am grateful for her interference; it would do us no good if I hurt them.

"Nate, I need to tell you something." She takes a deep breath. "Actually, I have something to tell all of you."

The waitress brings us all another round, I set my beer in front of Mariah in case she needs liquid courage. She takes it, downing a third in one gulp.

"Elizabeth is Elsie Williams," she says, her eyes not leaving Nate. "When you all shamed Colin for having a relationship with her all those years ago she left home. She landed a contract for all the books she has written." Mariah looks at me. "I was so proud of her." She takes another gulp. "I *am* so proud of her." Mariah amends. She turns her attention back to the others.

"That bitch is making money under our parent's name for her? Our last name?!" Daniel thunders. Marcus puts his arm out to hold his brother back from leaning too close to their sister.

"You wouldn't let her back to see our parents." She doesn't bother wiping her tears. "I was taking care of them and had student loans due, and I couldn't get either of you to pull your heads out of your ass long enough to help, I was alone." She hiccups. "Elizabeth hired me to be her assistant."

"We didn't need her to come home to help, there were nurses for Mom and Dad," Marcus insists.

"Elizabeth hired and paid for all the help our parents received." Mariah looks at Nate. "She has funded my entire life."

"How is she funding our lives? She is just a small-town writer."

"Our parents left us all trust funds; Elsie included. She took her monthly payments and used them to pay my student loan payments, our first apartment, our wedding. Everything is because of her. Look around you. This is not a small town! Elsie is a bona fide millionaire," Mariah yells! "Elsie writes romance, TV shows, and a few movies." She stops talking, her hands instantly cover her mouth. Her gaze lands on me in complete terror.

I have no time to think about what Mariah was telling the men at the table, her expression grips my attention. "What's wrong?" It is hard to keep the panic out of my voice.

"I have betrayed her." She falls against me in a fit of grief. Her sobs shaking her body.

I stroke her hair. "Everything will be okay," I try to soothe.

I look at the men at the table, all of them are still in varying states of shock. My phone goes off again and again. It takes a second to get to it now that Mariah is crying on me. "Yea?"

"Bradley." I hear my sister; her tone is guarded.

"What's up?" I try to sound conversational so that she isn't alarmed, and she doesn't alarm Mariah.

"Elsie is gone."

"What do you mean gone?" I whisper.

"I zoned out watching TV while she was writing. I heard her phone go off and she went into the bedroom. I thought maybe she had a meeting or something or went to the bathroom after her call so I didn't bother her." Natalie sounds out of breath, I hear her opening doors and calling for Elsie. "I got up to check on her and she's gone. Her phone is going straight to voicemail, her bag is here, her laptop is here, but she is gone." I hear her open a door and a click of maybe a light switch. "What's this?"

"What is it?" I hope she finds a note with a message like had to go to the front desk for a fax.

"There is a note here." I hear paper moving around on Natalie's end. I hear her sharp intake of breath, "Oh no."

"What?"

"There is a copy of our lawsuit for Death Burns Within and a paper signing over her rights to me for that series. She is LC Lucus." She is mumbling words, reading the rest of the note. "She says she loves us but that she can't risk anyone hurting us just because of who she is."

"What does that mean?" I growl.

"Give me a sec." I hear clicking and typing on her end. "I set up a group chat. A women's network, if you will. We will find her."

"A group chat?"

"Yea I put your public relations manager in it, her public relations manager, her editor, Elsie, and me." Natalie sounds impressed.

"I'm not even going to ask how you knew all that information and how you thought to do this." I would be impressed and proud of her if I wasn't trying to rein in my own imagination on where my fiancé was. "Natalie, is her ring with the note?" My heart drops to my stomach as I wait for her to answer.

"No. I don't see it anywhere." I have a sliver of hope.

"'Get me a flight to Ohio, now." I hang up. "Elsie is missing," I whisper to Mariah. "I'm going to get her and bring her back."

She looks up at me, her tearstained face now full of worry. "Elsie won't be found if she doesn't want to be." Her voice is a broken whisper.

"Trust me. Tell no one what I just said." I kiss the top of her head like I do with my own sister. "I don't want anyone to know my plans until I need them to."

Mariah nods before she disengages from me. My shirt has two wet pools on my chest where she poured her heart out.

"It was interesting meeting you all. I have a meeting early in the morning, so I will have to call it a night." I don't wait for any of them to answer me. The only thing I care about right now is making sure Elsie is safe and that she is never the only person on her team ever again.

"I know where she went." Mariah reaches out for me. "I'm coming with you."

I shake my head. "You have a wedding to get ready for."

"No." Mariah's voice is loud. As if the entire room went silent at my statement and was waiting for her reaction. "I will cancel the wedding. It isn't my wedding anyway." She turns to point at the small group of men still standing around the table, all sobering up in record time. "Those assholes made my special day all about themselves, like they always do." Mariah links her arm through mine. "Let's go find my sister."

Nate doesn't utter a word and neither do either of her brothers. I nod and lead her out of the bar to the elevators. I swipe my card to take us up to the penthouse.

Natalie meets us at the elevator; she is pacing and checking her phone. "Cole is coming to gather everything from the penthouse and take it back to your house for now." She is clicking away as we try to make a plan.

"I know where Elsie went, let's get in my car and go get her." Mariah tugs on my arm, attempting to pull me back to the elevator.

"Type the address into my phone, I will go get her. I pat her hand that is still on my arm. "I won't let anything happen to her. I promise." I offer Mariah a small smile as I hand her my phone.

Mariah takes it, and I leave her to her task. "Natalie, I need to see the lawsuit. I don't know why that might have triggered her to bolt."

My sister hands me the papers from the lawyer for my company. I feel both women step closer to read the document too. I shake my head, "I don't see anything on here that makes any sense."

Mariah's phone rings. "Sasha?" She glances at us, "Elsie's publisher." She holds up her finger for us. "Yes?" Hitting the speaker button, she answers, "Yes?"

"Has Elsie spoken to you about the series contracts, I sent them to her less than an hour ago?" The woman on the other end sounds exasperated.

"Not that I can remember. Why?" Mariah's brow furrows.

"Miller-Works Productions has proceeded with a court case trying to retain rights to *Death Burns Within*. They are claiming Elsie is the heiress to their company and as such she has a legal and moral obligation to let their production company have her series."

"Fuck." Mariah whispers. "I have to go. I will call you back." She hangs up without saying anything else.

"They have no legal grounds!" Natalie yells as she resumes firing off texts or emails of her own. My sister stabs the down button for the elevator then resumes her flurry of typing.

CHAPTER 54

*E*LSIE

Natalie and I fall into a comfortable silence as we watch a reality show about finding love. I decide to put my food away for later, as I wander into the kitchen, I see the envelopes on the counter Natalie had brought up with the food. Both are addressed to me but from different people; the labels are totally different. My phone goes off in my pocket. I make my way to the bedroom, envelopes under my arm as I answer the phone. I note it is an Ohio area code.

"Hello, I am looking for an Elizabeth or Elsie Williams," a young woman's voice is on the other end of my phone line.

"This is Elizabeth, how can I help you?"

"Yes, hello, I am calling on behalf of Evaline Miller. She is currently in the hospital and would like to speak to you do you have a moment?"

My heart aches a little more thinking about that kind old woman all alone in the hospital. "Of course I have a few minutes."

"Thank you, one moment while I transfer the call to her room." The line goes silent before a tone trills. As I wait, I open one of the envelopes I had brought into the bedroom with me. It's a lawsuit for copyright infringement for *Death Burns Within* vs *Annex*. I smile to myself as I sit it on the desk in front of me. The next envelope is a letter from Miller Works Productions. Looking over the document I can deduce they are attempting to stop the TV series deals coming my way for *Death Burns Within* and are demanding they have rights as they believe I am a long-lost family member. I can't help the eyeroll that accompanies the reading of that letter.

"Miss?" The young woman is back on the phone. "Yes, thank you for holding, Evaline is asleep right now. I will let her know she can contact you when she has a moment. Thank you again for waiting on the line." She hangs up before I can ask any questions or say another word to her.

I slip my phone back into the back pocket of my jeans as my gaze lands on the lawsuit on the desk and back to the letter in my hand from Miller Works Productions and a brilliant idea strikes me. Before I can get my document printed from my computer my phone chimes again. Instinctually, I pull out my phone and open the text message.

'We need to talk. How much have you been hiding?' The message is from Marcus. My stomach drops. 'I'm on my way to see you now.' My heart breaks knowing I have been betrayed. I'm not ready to reinvent myself, to leave everyone I have in my life behind.

As quick as I can I grab a piece of paper and write out my plan to Natalie. Without taking anything but my small purse I make my way as fast and quietly as I can. I don't want Natalie to stop me from my escape. I don't have a moment to lose; Marcus is on his way here. The last time he was alone with me he tried to hold me under water in the backyard pool. A shiver runs down my spine. The man hates me, always has. I take a deep breath as I make it to the elevator, push the lobby button, and wait for the doors to open so I can make a run for it.

My fight or flight is in full panic mode. I take a deep breath as I make my way outside and start walking. I pull out my phone to grab an uber. I need to stop at my rented house to grab my things before I head to the airport to get home. I put an email in to the realtor that sold my house to me two years ago and got me the rental here. Time to make a clean break of it all. As I type my attention is caught by the glittering from the ring on my finger. My heart breaks a little more. I don't want to lose what I have found with Bradley. Another chime comes in.

'Where are you, Bitch?!' Another text from Marcus.

I check and make sure the car and driver match the app before I put my phone on airplane mode. I slide it into my purse and relax in the car as we make the thirty-minute trip to my rental. My head pounding from all the little things I am making a note to change or cancel and my heart mourning the loss of the only man who ever treated me like I mattered. *He betrayed you.* My mind reminds me. I refuse to cry in the car with a stranger. It takes no time to get to the rental. The driver parks in front of the house for me to get out.

"Could you stay and take me to the airport, too? I can pay you cash double what you would have been paid. It will only take me a couple of minutes to grab the rest of my things."

"Sure. I can do that." He offers a smile.

"Great. Thanks. Be out in just a few minutes." I hop out of the car and rush to the front door. As I close the door the first tear escapes my eye. I carry myself to the small bedroom and collapse on top of the bed, my pain overflowing and crippling me. For the first time in a long time, I allow myself to feel every ounce of it. I let myself feel the loss and loneliness. The what could have beens, the what ifs, and the if onlys swirl in my mind.

CHAPTER 55

BRADLEY

The doors open for us to go down to our cars. "Legalities don't matter. They will use their clout to keep her series buried until Elsie either gives in and does what they want, or she abandons that series. If she were to make any other series, they would do the same thing." Mariah shakes her head, as she steps into the elevator, Natalie and I follow. "That is why she ran. That is what she is protecting you from." Mariah looks at me, tears brim her eyes. "There isn't anything I can think to do to help her."

My head is a jumble of thoughts and ideas, but one thing is crystal clear. I smile at Mariah. "I have a plan." I tap my sister on the shoulder. "I need you to meet me at the office in an hour. Keep trying to get ahold of Elsie." I turn back to Mariah. "You too. Keep trying to get ahold of her. Go with Natalie to the office. I will be there shortly. Take her laptop to Shane, see if there is anything on there that can help us get some answers."

Mariah and Natalie both nod; and the doors open to the main lobby of the hotel. The women make their way outside. I pull out my phone and open the navigation app. The address Mariah had typed in is only thirty minutes from the hotel. My mind went on autopilot following the navigation in silence. I am hoping against all hope that I will get to the house before she disappears forever. The navigation as me turning onto her street, my breath catches as I see a car sitting outside the house I am pulling up to.

I throw my car in park and rush to the driver window of the other car. There is a young man in the driver seat, and I tap on the window and take a step back waiting for him to roll it down. It feels like minutes tick by as he cracks the window.

"Can I help you?" He eyes me warily.

"Thank you for bringing my wife home, you are welcome to stick around but I don't think your service will be needed." I pull out my wallet and give the young guy a hundred before I wave to him as I run to the front door. I instinctively try to open the front door and find it unlocked. I lock the door behind me and listen for Elsie. Her sobs are muffled but they seem to reverberate within my heart.

"Else?" I keep my tone soft, but I don't want to startle her as I walk toward the bedroom. Her sobs intensify. The door is easy to push open. Elsie laying across the bed, her sobs wrecking her body looks nothing like those Disney princesses my sister made me watch growing up. I almost laugh at my wayward thought. Almost.

Three steps is what it takes for me to make it from the doorway to Elsie's bed. "Else." I pull her to me as I sit on the side of the bed. Her arms come around my middle. "It will be okay, baby." I smooth her hair as she tries to regain control of her sadness. "I got you, I won't let anything happen to you." I kiss the top of her hair.

"Betrayed." Is all I can make out at first. Her sobs have hindered her breathing. She holds me tighter, "Marcus."

My heart drops to my stomach. She wants Marcus? My brain recalls the proud looking blonde from the bar earlier. It takes me a hot moment to realize Elsie is panicking. Her breathing is three to my one. I try to move her so she is looking at me. "Breathe with me, Else." I stroke her hair, giving up on moving her while she is in this state.

"He's coming for me." Her tone bordering on hysteria. "I have to get out of here."

"Elsie!" My voice sharp as I try to command her attention. "Look at me."

She stops fighting me finally and looks up at me. Her eyes still have tears in them, but her face is full of fear.

"I won't let anyone hurt you. Do you hear me?" I situate us so we are both laying on top of the bed.

Elsie's breathing eventually slows. Her arm still draped over my stomach, her head on my shoulder. "I need to leave," she finally says. Her voice no louder than a whisper.

"Mariah didn't mean to spill your secret." I keep my arm around her. "I think she just was so overwhelmed and stressed over her wedding going off the rails because her family took over." Elsie doesn't say anything. "Though I wish you could have seen their faces when they heard her tirade." I chuckle.

Elsie disengages from me to sit up. I watch as she looks around the room, slowly taking everything in. "I need to pack," she states as she slowly stands up. I watch as she pulls open the top drawer of the dresser. She pulls out a small pile of folded clothes and deposits them into a small carryon on the floor near the door. She has everything packed within fifteen minutes.

I stand up to put myself between her and the door out of the room. "Elsie, I have an idea."

I wait for her to look up at me with those striking limestone eyes. "I need you to trust me. I have a plan." I walk to her and take her carryon out of her hand. I set it down and take both her hands in mine. "I love you, Else."

Elsie searches my face for what feels like hours. Finally, I hear the exact thing I needed to hear from the woman I love. "I love you, too. I trust you. What is the plan?"

I can't help the smile that overcomes me as I bend to kiss Elsie with all the passion and love I can convey.

CHAPTER 56

THE DAY OF MARIAH'S WEDDING

BRADLEY

"Glad you could make it!" I open the door of my penthouse to Nate, moving out of the way for him to walk in.

"Yea, I have time to kill before the ceremony." His tone is somber. "I'm not sure she is going to show up. She is still pretty pissed off at me."

"Would you accompany me down to the VIP lounge? My company is having a meeting and I have to make an appearance for a moment and then we can go get a drink at the bar."

"Yea. Sure, no problem." We walk together to the elevators. I swipe my keycard to access the VIP lounge.

"I would get a drink in the lounge, but I really don't want to stick around for the conclusion of the meeting." I offer him a half smile. Nate nods as he steps out to the floor of the lounge.

"Hey! There he is!" Daniel calls holding up a flute of bubbly.

"Hey, man!" Nate calls and walks towards Daniel, Marcus, and Colin. All are standing over at the bar. "Why are you here?"

"We are waiting for the meeting to start." Marcus' voice is louder than it needs to be. "This is it, boys!" Marcus downs his drink, "Easy street!" He holds out the glass for the bartender to refill.

Nate's gaze flits to me before the other men's. "What is he doing here?" Colin spits out, his tone icy. There's my queue.

"Welcome, ladies and gentlemen. If I could have your attention, we will start this most anticipated meeting." Natalie's voice calls over the speakers. The men with Nate all look around proudly as the cameras and videographers encircling the small gathering. "It is my pleasure to introduce Derrick Derrickson, the owner and creator of *Annex*." She holds out her hand, and the crowd parts. I make my way to her. I take the microphone from her as I replace her on the dais.

"Good afternoon!" I look around the room of the fifty or so people around me. "I would like to welcome you all to the announcement of the most anticipated expansion and cinematic venture ever to rock Derrickson Entertainment." I wait for the applause to die back down. "First, I need to address the acquisition of *Death Burns Within*." I smile at my sister, Natalie. "We are excited to incorporate the lore of *Death Burns Within* in our next expansion. Hopefully, the micro expansion rolling out this weekend will keep fans happy and engaged for the foreseeable future."

"Speaking of engaged, I would like to take this opportunity to introduce to you all to my wife." From behind the curtain my Elsie comes out to stand next to me. "Elizabeth and I were married last night. She not only is a best-selling author, known as Elsie Williams; but she is also L C Lucus. The creator of *Death Burns Within*." I squeeze her hand, she squeezes back. "She will be staying on as our series writer." I lean down to kiss her. "Now, about the cinematic fans have been clamoring for!" I again wait for the chatter and applause to quiet. "We have struck a deal to make the movie a reality."

I watch as the men in the back stand a little straighter; they all look around the room anticipating recognition. "While we had been in talks with DMCN Productions we have decided that we don't see eye to eye on moral and ethical stances and have decided instead to go with Miller Works Productions since my wife's family owns it."

You could hear a pin drop as the entire room fell silent. "That fucking whore!" I hear one of Mariah's brother's bellow.

"Security, could you please escort the production team of DMCN out of the building." I smile as the men's anger turn to shock. "Nate." I call out. The microphone amplifies my voice perfectly. "This is it man. The moment you have to make a decision." The crowd once again parts as Nate turns to look at me. "Which team are you on?"

Nate looks from me to the men behind him being shown out by security. He takes entirely too long to answer, I almost tell him 'time's up' and let him accept his fate, but I feel Elizabeth's hand on my arm. "Give him a minute." She looks up at me. "He has to come to terms with what you are saying. That's his family, too."

Mariah comes to stand beside Elsie. Her choice clearly made. Nate takes slow deliberate steps up to the dais to pull Mariah to him in a tight hug. "Will you still have me?"

Mariah looks up at the man she was made for, their story written and waiting for them. "Of course." I watch as Elsie smiles softly, her gaze only on me.

"We have a wedding to get you to." Elsie whispers to her sister.

"Thank you all for coming, I hope you all enjoy the luncheon." I offer my arm to my wife as Nate takes Mariah's hand. We exit the lounge to make our way out to my car so we can make it to the plane.

"I think we are going to be late to our own wedding." Mariah laughs as we park.

"I might have changed the plans a bit," I keep my tone light and proceed with caution, " We are taking my own plane."

"To Ohio...?" Mariah stops to really look at me.

"We are all going to Vegas." Elsie's tone is full of excitement and she grabs Mariah's hands in hers.

Mariah eyes widen as she swivels her gaze from Elsie to me.

You can see the apprehension fade off her as the excitement replaces it just as fast.

"Seriously?" Nate gives us the widest grin.

Realization dawns on Mariah, "Oh Elsie! Just like in the story!"

"I told Bradley how your story ends. He said it was too perfect not to make it your reality." Elsie hugged her sister before we all started for the terminal.

We get into the air and on our way with no issues. Sometimes having my own jet is worth it. We try to only use it sparingly but this seems like a great reason. When we are in the air for a bit I finally have time to talk to my wife. "When you ran I sent your laptop to my brother to look for clues so I could find you." I wait to continue to gauge her reaction. When she turned to look at me all she showed was patience. I continued, "there is a full manuscript on there, that shows you had been working on it the whole time you were in the penthouse with me."

"Yes, I wrote for almost an entire day or even two." She pursed her lips, "That isn't unusual."

"I thought you were done with your Kismet Summer series." My fingers found hers.

"I wrote what my perfect proposal, my dream for myself and the hope for my future." Her voice was soft but her honestly was profound.

"What are your dreams, my love?" I resisted pressing my lips to hers.

Her eyes searched mine for a long moment. "My reality is so much better than I could ever imagine." Her lips found mine as her hands cradled my face. Her pure honesty resonated in her words and actions more than anything I have experienced in my thirty-one years on earth.

CHAPTER 57

*E*LSIE

"How did you get Miller Works Production to stop their lawsuit?" Natalie turns to wait for my asnswer.

"Well, remember Evaline?" I look at Mariah and try to stifle my laugh at her furrowed brows. "The old woman in Ohio who called me and you told me I talked too much?" Marish nodded as realization washed over her. "Well, turns out she is my grandmother. My mother had me and decided she was not ready to be a mother so she put me up for adoption. The first family that adopted me got into a horrible accident and it left me with no one so I ended up in fostercare. I was there from age four until I aged out. Apparently, Evaline has been searching and paying private detectives for years. When she finally got a lead and I kept refusing the DNA tests she decided to call and see if I would talk to her." I shrug, "The rest is history."

"Just like that?" Natalie's voice is full of awe and her eyes are wide in wonder.

"No, but honestly, after I talked to her and really sat and thought about it I realized Evaline and I were both lonely and missing connections. I decided to give her the benefit of the doubt. We thought up the plan to let Miller Works Production and Derrikson Entertainment both work on Death Burns Within. Evaline is happy, Bradley is happy, and I'm happy that everything seems to be going better than I could expect. I lean my head on Bradley's shoulder as I let myself drift off to a dreamless sleep. Dreamless because nothing in my dreams will ever be better than what I am living right now.

ABOUT THE AUTHOR

I present to you, Darling Reader, in no particular order a few things about myself. I have been clinically dead on three separate occasions. My social anxiety is more severe than a ginger without sunscreen getting too close to a window on a partially cloudy day. I have lived in three countries. I'm an adrenaline junkie. I have four children. My entire existence is fueled by adrenaline and spite. Secretly, I watch Hallmark movies when my family goes to sleep. I have cuddled a tiger. I have fifteen siblings. I have difficulty creating memories. My favorite book is <u>To Kill a Mockingbird</u>.

Now, my darling reader, I will now inform you, there are eight truths and three lies within my narrative. Best of luck in your deductions my friend!